BULLETS FOR A BADMAN

BULLETS FOR A BADMAN

Bennett Foster

Chivers Press • G.K. Hall & Co.
Bath, England Thorndike, Maine USA

Original title: *Winter Quarters.*
Serialized version (*Western Story* Magazine) July to August, 1942.

This Large Print edition is published by Chivers Press, England, and by G.K. Hall & Co., USA.

Published in 1998 in the U.K. by arrangement with Golden West Literary Agency.

Published in 1998 in the U.S. by arrangement with Golden West Literary Agency.

U.K. Hardcover ISBN 0–7540–3127–6 (Chivers Large Print)
U.S. Softcover   ISBN 0–7838–8291–2 (Nightingale Collection Edition)

Set in 16 pt. New Times Roman.

Printed in Great Britain on acid-free paper.

British Library Cataloguing in Publication Data available

Library of Congress Cataloging-in-Publication Data

Foster, Bennett.
  Bullets for a badman / Bennett Foster.
    p. cm.
  ISBN 0–7838–8291–2 (large print : sc : alk. paper)
  1. Large type books. I. Title.
[PS3511.O6812B85 1998]
813′.54—dc21   97–35650

CHAPTER ONE

Dan Mar's face had been carved from the same piece of saddle leather as his father's. He had the same level brows, the same blue eyes, and the same obstinate chin, and when he scowled the resemblance was startling. Clara Mar, carrying the coffeepot between the stove and kitchen table, was struck, as always, by the similarity. To see Dan and Bruce together, she thought, was like watching a man grow up. The years had carved a personality on Bruce's face, deepening lines and wrinkles that Dan's did not have. Otherwise the men were prototypes.

They were alike in temperament too—Clara stifled a sigh as she filled her husband's cup—obstinate, forceful, clinging to an idea even after they had been proven wrong. Sometimes she wished that Bruce were less forceful, for Dan's pliability lessened as he grew older, and recently she had been hard put to keep the peace. They were at it again this morning, arguing. Dan would give in, but someday would come the one hot word that led to open rebellion, and then what could she do?

'It's not time to turn out,' Bruce stated. 'March is too early. I've seen blizzards in May, an' because grass has come early this year is no reason to take a chance.'

'We've fed most of our hay'—Dan's jaw was

obstinate—'an' there's green grass two inches tall scattered all through the old grass. They'd do well on that, an' if it came on to storm we could get them in.'

Bruce drank coffee. 'They're still my cattle,' he stated, putting down the cup, 'an' it's still my outfit. We won't turn out till I think it's safe.'

So these controversies always ended: with Bruce flatly declaring his ownership. Clara looked swiftly from her son to her husband. Dan was a good boy and obedient, but she knew how Bruce's calm assumption of authority rankled. It rankled in her own quiet mind. After all, Dan did most of the real work at the MY, the hard riding, the greater part of the winter feeding; and in the summer it was Dan who ran the hay crews. But Bruce spoke of the cattle as 'my cattle' and the MY as 'my ranch,' admitting neither his wife nor his son to partnership.

Bruce wiped his lips and got up. 'What have you got in mind for today?' he asked, taking for granted that the argument was finished.

Dan lifted his easy height from the chair. He was a little taller than his father and not so heavy; in so much their resemblance ceased.

'I thought I'd ride the east pasture,' the boy answered. 'Ruffin has turned out his stock and I haven't been along that fence.'

Bruce paused in the act of putting on his coat. 'Don't go to Ruffin's,' he ordered. 'I

2

don't want you over there.'

A sullen, resentful look came to Dan's face. 'I've never run into anything wrong at Tom Ruffin's,' he said. 'You don't like me to go over there because of the show people.'

'I don't like to have you runnin' with folks that are no good,' Bruce stated flatly. 'Those show hands ain't our kind. The men don't amount to nothin', an' the women...'

'Tom Ruffin don't amount to much?' Dan interrupted. 'He's got the best outfit in this part of the state. He's president of the Stockman's Bank in Brule. He was state senator. He...'

'Oh, Tom!' Bruce waved aside Dan's protest. 'Tom's all right. He was always a showman an' he can't help it. But don't you forget that Tom Ruffin was mixed up in the Mitchell business. It was never proved that he hired Mitchell, but when Mitchell was tried for murder Ruffin stood up for him.'

'He sticks by his friends,' Dan retorted. 'That's not a bad thing to do. I like Tom Ruffin an' so do you. You always have.'

'Everybody likes Tom,' Bruce admitted. 'But the rest of 'em...'

'Then what about Carl Thwaite and Penny?' Dan interposed. 'They're good people.'

'Carl'—Bruce paused beside the door— 'might have been all right. He had a good start in the cow business when his father died. Then he went with Ruffin's show. He sold the old place and the cattle his daddy had worked a

3

long time gettin'. I used to think a lot of Carl but I don't now. An' his sister's just as bad. She's a good enough girl, I guess, but I can't see her in a kitchen like this, doin' the things your mother does. She's been spoiled. You stay away from Ruffin's, Dan. I won't have you over there.' The door closed behind Bruce's broad back.

Dan, his coat buttoned, pulled on his gloves. He was scowling, and his mother knew that he was angry. She put an apple and two cinnamon rolls into a small sack and brought it to her son. 'You mustn't mind what your father says, Dan,' she said. 'It's just that he wants the best for you.'

'There's no need of him ripping into Penny,' Dan growled. 'He treats me like a kid. I'm twenty-one years old an' I haven't any more to say about what I do than I did ten years ago. He won't pay me wages, and every time I make a suggestion I'm wrong. It's not too early to turn the cattle out. I've fed for two hours today already, an' now I've got to feed some more an' then go ride that fence.' Automatically the boy put his lunch in the pocket of his sheepskin.

'But he thinks so much of you, son,' Clara pleaded. 'He's proud of you, and he had such a hard time himself when he was young. You've heard him tell about it. And he did give you the money for those calves last year. You know he did.'

'An' put it in a savings account so that I

couldn't get it!' Dan rasped. 'I know that he started followin' a wagon when he was twelve; I've heard him tell about it often enough. He was lucky. They paid him what he earned. There's nothing wrong with Carl Thwaite, Mother, an' Penny's the nicest girl in this country. But I can't even talk to 'em because they're show people!' Dan stamped angrily to the door. 'I get mighty tired of bein' treated like a kid!'

Outside the house the wind blew, brisk and cold, sending small clouds racing across the sky. Dan, walking to the corral, could see his father, mounted on a big gray horse, topping the rise beyond the barn. Bruce Mar rode straight up and down, easy as a youngster, and when the bay horse crowhopped a jump or two, Bruce sat him. Despite his anger, Dan felt a thrill of pride. Bruce, fifty-five years old, could ride and handle cattle with any man.

Dan led his young horse, Domino, out of the pen and stopped at the saddle shed to slip a Winchester into the scabbard on his saddle, anticipating a possible shot at a coyote. Domino snorted and rolled his eyes and said plainly that he was going to buck. But Dan Mar had never seen a horse that he wouldn't try to ride and very few that he couldn't ride. He climbed aboard the appaloosa, rode a few short jumps, and, pulling Domino's head up, trotted off.

By midmorning Dan had finished feeding

5

and was riding fence in the east pasture. At a corner where the fence turned north, just beyond a gate, he found the wire down and plain sign of cattle that had gone through. Dismounting, Dan hobbled Domino and fell to work with staples and fence pliers, almost glad that the wire was down, for it offered a release for the angry energy that filled him. He had pulled all four wires tight and was tacking the top strand when riders came over the ridge. Dan put in the last staple and straightened as the riders came abreast.

'Hello, kid.' Carl Thwaite reined in his big horse. 'Fixin' a little fence this mornin'?'

Dan grinned. He liked and admired Carl. 'Some,' he answered. 'Hello, Penny.'

The golden-haired girl smiled. She sat her big black horse with the ease and grace of a woman who had spent more time in the saddle than on foot, and the horse, high-headed, groomed until he shone, set off her accomplishment.

'Good morning, Dan,' she answered. 'You're out early. I suppose you've done a day's work by now?'

Dan grinned, for the MY had a reputation for early rising. 'Not quite,' he answered. 'Just half a day. The rest of the day I'm goin' to spend gettin' Ruffin's cattle out of our pasture.'

'There *was* a few went through,' Carl drawled, looking at the tracks. 'Tell you what,

Dan. Penny an' me'll help you get 'em out if you'll come over and ride Dusty for me. I want to get in a little practice.'

Temptation prodded Dan and he hesitated an instant. Then: 'I'll go you one on that,' he answered, deliberately flouting his father's orders. 'Go on to the gate and come through. I'll see if I can pick up Ruffin's cows.'

'O.K.' Carl Thwaite rode down the fence toward the gate.

The three had no difficulty in locating the cattle that had gone through the fence or in putting them back where they belonged. With the job finished, the men, Penny between them, rode on toward Ruffin's headquarters.

Ruffin had established himself close against a bluff that edged a long flat. To the north was Turkey Mountain and beyond that the rough country around Vinegar Creek, once the property of the Thwaites. Ruffin's two-storied white house was outlined against the towering bluff in the background and flanked by three smaller cottages used during the winter season by performers who stayed at the ranch. Below the house were the barns and corrals, and set at right angles to these were the bunkhouse and cookhouse used by the ranch crew and such unmarried men as wintered with Tom Ruffin. In front of the corrals and the bunkhouse was an oval arena smoothly graded and enclosed with a white fence. Ruffin himself, his eyes twinkling, walked out from the arena as Dan and the Thwaites rode up.

'Hello, Dan,' Ruffin greeted. 'Come over to sign up for the season?'

Dan liked Ruffin, his shrewdness, his friendliness, his innate showmanship. Tom Ruffin operated one of the biggest Wild West shows in the business and, coupled with the show, sent a string of race horses to the minor tracks during the racing season. Added to these was his ranch. Not quite fifty, Tom Ruffin was a widower, wealthy, a power in state politics.

'I might take a job with the cow outfit,' Dan answered.

'Have to see Buck about punchin' cows,' Ruffin retorted. Buck Ruffin, Tom's son, ran the ranch and cattle. 'I guess Buck would put you on.'

Dan laughed, for he and Buck Ruffin had gone to school together and were friends. 'I came over,' he said, 'to ride that new horse Carl is breakin' for his act. What's the matter, Tom? Haven't you got any horsemen on your place?'

'Plenty,' Ruffin returned. 'But if Carl wants *you* he wants *you*. Hello, Smokey.'

Smokey Darnell, slender and darkly handsome, came up and stopped by the two men, nodding to Dan, who briefly returned the greeting. Darnell and his wife, Belle, formed one of the two roping acts that Ruffin carried with his show. They were good, Dan admitted grudgingly, but not as good as Penny and Carl Thwaite.

'Here's Dusty, Dan,' Carl called. 'Want to change your saddle to him?' Carl was in the arena holding a big white horse.

'Sure,' Dan agreed, and went to Domino, Ruffin and Darnell following casually.

'That's quite a horse you've got there,' Ruffin remarked, eying Domino. 'He'd make a show horse. Want to sell him?'

Domino hung back on the reins and rolled his eyes as Dan reached for the latigo. 'Nope,' Dan answered. 'He ain't got sense enough to make a show horse.'

'An' anyhow,' Darnell drawled, 'old Bruce Mar wouldn't sell a horse to a show. You know that.' Darnell laughed.

'Domino's mine.' Dan pulled the saddle off and carried it and his rifle to the fence.

When Dusty was saddled Dan tried the horse, riding him back and forth across the arena, reining and stopping. In a trick roping act it is essential that the horse stop the instant he is caught, otherwise the rider might get hurt. Carl Thwaite was training Dusty to replace an older horse, and while Penny would ride the horse in the act, Carl did not trust her with Dusty's training. Thwaite rolled out his rope, gathered it, and swung a loop. 'All right,' he called. 'The forelegs this time.'

Dan brought Dusty up at a run; the loop shot out and settled, and Dusty squatted on his hind feet.

'That's O.K.,' Carl called.

9

Dan rode past again, and Carl, spinning his rope, jumped through and back, rolled out his loop, and caught Dusty's front legs and head. Practice was as necessary for the man as for the horse. Almost every day when the show was in winter quarters the performers worked at their acts, sharpening their timing, keeping muscles smooth and supple. Their artistry depended upon physical perfection, and they dared not let themselves relax. Thwaite was a pretty roper. Every move looked easy and effortless, but at the end of ten minutes he was breathing hard and called a respite.

'You take the rope awhile, Dan. Let me take Dusty.'

Nothing loath, Dan dismounted. There was a little crowd at the arena fence. Belle Darnell had joined her husband, and Nevada Warren stood beside Belle. Some of the other performers were present. Captain Purrington, who did a shooting act with the show, and Red Halsey, the bronc rider, were perched on the fence beside three or four others. Dan took the rope and shook it out, and Carl, mounting Dusty, rode to the end of the arena.

Any kind of roping would have sufficed, for the purpose was to train the horse; but Dan Mar was no ordinary roper. As a boy, playing with Buck Ruffin, he had seen the best trick ropers in the business and had practiced rope work hour after hour, sometimes profiting by an amused word of advice given by a master.

10

This was not all, for one summer a *vaquero* from Old Mexico had worked in the hay at the MY. The Mexican had been raised in Sonora, that land of good ropers, and from him Dan had learned some fancy catches. Now, as Carl rode Dusty back and forth, Dan called his shots and played with the rope, dancing through it, spinning it, and making it come alive. Perhaps his exhibition was not so finished as Carl Thwaite's, not so graceful, but it was good. Very good.

Carl rode over to the fence, his eyes bright. 'That's enough for this mornin',' he said.

Dan coiled the rope. 'Looks like he'd do,' Dan agreed.

'Yo're wastin' talent, Danny,' Ruffin commented. 'I'll pay you a hundred a month an' your chuck this summer. Why don't you come along?'

Dan shook his head. 'No. I guess not, Tom.'

'Good ropin'.' Smokey Darnell's voice was smooth. 'Of course it's a little different ropin' here in front of friends an' doin' it for an audience.' There was a casual inflection in the man's voice that made the hair lift on the back of Dan Mar's neck. He didn't like Smokey Darnell, never had.

'I don't know,' Dan answered coolly. 'I never thought trick ropin' was so hard. There's things that can be done with a rope that are a lot harder than spinnin' it an' catchin' a horse.'

'Such as?' Darnell challenged.

Dan shrugged. 'Lots of things.'

'Well,' Smokey Darnell laughed. 'I catch three horses abreast in my act. Spin the loop, jump it twice, an' catch 'em. That's hard enough. Let's see you do that, Mar.'

'I'll do that,' Dan answered the challenge, 'if you'll do what I do, Darnell.'

'I expect I can do anything you can do. Want to bet a little, Mar? I'll bet a hundred dollars against that appaloosa horse that I match anythin' you do.'

It was a challenge, and Dan rose to it. 'I'll take that,' he agreed. 'Tom, have you got a steer in the pens?'

'We run in a bunch this mornin',' Red Halsey announced. 'Smokey, I'll take another hundred of yore money if you want to bet it. Dan's a cowhan'. He can do stuff with a rope you show han's never seen.'

'That's a bet,' Darnell answered. 'Bring out your steer.'

'I'd like to use Nigger,' Dan said. 'How about it?'

Ruffin nodded, and Red Halsey came down from the fence. 'I'll get him while they fetch the steer,' he said, and hurried off across the arena.

'What are you going to do, Dan?' Penny leaned across the fence and spoke low-voiced. 'You know Smokey Darnell can rope circles around you. What kind of foolishness is this?'

'Not foolishness,' Dan answered quietly. 'Carl, I want to use your long rope.'

12

'Help yourself, Dan.' Carl Thwaite's face was serious. 'I don't know what yo're up to, kid, but I'm afraid you've lost a horse.'

'We'll see.' Dan turned away from Penny and her brother and began to unsaddle Dusty. From the stable Red was leading Nigger, big and black, and wise as Satan, and a cowboy came from the corral driving a red steer.

Dan mounted Nigger and tried the horse. The steer was in the arena, big and long-horned and glaring belligerently at the spectators. Satisfied with the horse, Dan asked for the rope and, when it was handed him, fell to tying a slip knot in the free end.

'I want you to run that steer for me, Carl,' he said casually. 'When I catch him drop back.'

'Sure,' Carl answered. 'But what are you going to do, kid?'

'Catch the steer.' Dan put his slip noose around his neck and pulled it up. What he proposed now was apparent. With the end of the rope around his neck he would catch the steer, dally and stop the animal. If anything went wrong, if the dallies slipped on his saddle horn, if the steer hit the end of the rope before he could dally, Dan would be jerked down and dragged, choked by the rope.

'You can't do that, kid!' Carl Thwaite gasped.

'Can't I?' Dan answered. 'Watch me! If you don't want to haze for me, I'll get Red to do it.'

Thwaite shook his head and turned away.

13

'I'll haze,' he said. Dan rode Nigger toward the far end of the arena, and Carl mounted.

The steer, with Carl hazing, started at a lumbering run. Nigger, seeing the rope swinging over his head, jumped forward, coming down like lightning on the red steer. The rope flashed out, and Dan's hand was a blur as he took his dallies. The steer hit the end of the rope and Nigger sat down, while Dan Mar played the big red animal as a man might play a trout, giving and taking rope, the dallies tight around his saddle horn. The steer fought, choked, bellowed, and when the time was right Dan Mar went past and threw the animal, dropping from his saddle to run forward and kneel on the weaving red neck. He held the steer down a minute and then, freeing his rope, ran back, jumped on Nigger, and rode toward the fence. The steer, scrambling up, stood a moment, head low, and then, with enough of that kind of nonsense, trotted toward the far end of the arena.

'All right, Darnell,' Dan said quietly, dismounting beside the fence. 'Do that and I'll hand you Domino.'

Smokey Darnell's face was flushed. 'That ain't trick ropin',' he protested. 'That's just damned foolishness. Any man that will do that is crazy. I meant I'd match any kind of trick ropin' you did. I won't be a big enough fool to try a stunt like that.'

'Then'—Dan's voice was even quieter after

14

Darnell's bluster—'I'll take a hundred dollars of your money.'

'An' I'll take a hundred,' Red Halsey announced. 'If that wasn't ropin', I never seen it. Pay off, Smokey.'

'Dan, you young fool!' That was Carl Thwaite. 'If ever I see you do a thing like that again, I'll...'

'You'll not see it, Thwaite.' The voice, deep, rasping, stopped Carl's words. Every man and woman along the fence turned to look at the speaker. Bruce Mar, on his big bay, sat and stared at them.

'Get on your horse, Dan,' Bruce ordered, 'an' go home. You've got no business here.'

CHAPTER TWO

Dan made no move to obey, and Bruce glared at his son. 'I told you to get your horse!' he snapped.

'I heard you!' Dan's eyes were as hard and as angry as his father's.

Anger clashed with anger and iron-hard will with a resolution equally adamant. 'Either,' Bruce said levelly, 'you get on yore horse an' come now or you don't need to come at all.'

There was no question in the mind of any listener that Bruce Mar meant exactly what he said. Either Dan obeyed the order given or he was done at the MY. For just an instant indecision tore at Dan and then, deliberately, he turned to Tom Ruffin. 'You offered me a job a while ago. I'll take it.'

Without a word Bruce rode toward the gate, reaching it before anyone spoke. Then Tom Ruffin said: 'He meant that, Dan. It ain't too late to catch him.'

Dan's face was stony hard. 'An' I meant what I said. I'm not goin' to catch him. The thing that interests me is, did you mean it when you offered me a job, or were you foolin'?'

Ruffin was on a spot. He did not really want Dan Mar with the show, for he had two good rope acts. But he had made the offer, although in jest, and before all these others he would not back down. 'Yo're on the payroll when the show starts,' he answered. 'If you want it that way.'

'I want it that way.'

Silence held for an instant and then Ruffin growled: 'Put up the stock. Dan, you come up to the house.'

The tension was broken. Red Halsey took Nigger's reins and said, 'I'll unsaddle for you, Dan. Want me to put yore appaloosa in the corral or turn him out?'

'Turn him out,' Dan answered. 'Thanks, Red.' Ruffin was walking toward the house, and Dan hurried to join him. Carl Thwaite spoke to one of the men on the fence and followed Dan and Ruffin.

16

In the big front room Ruffin put on a pair of spectacles and fumbled in a drawer of his desk. 'We'll make out a contract, Dan,' he announced. 'I told you a hundred. That right?'

'That's right, Tom.'

Ruffin sat down at the desk and his pen scratched. Carl Thwaite came in, and Ruffin glanced up over his spectacles.

'Dan,' Carl said quietly, 'you want to think about this. Yore father needs you on the place. He can't swing it alone.'

'I have thought about it,' Dan snapped. 'He'll have to hire somebody.'

Ruffin had finished filling out the contract. He pushed it across the desk. 'Sign right there,' he directed.

Dan took the pen.

'Wait,' Carl ordered. 'Where are you goin' to use Dan, Tom?'

Ruffin looked at Carl and then at Dan. 'I can use him ridin' broncs, if no place else,' he replied. 'He's a pretty rider an' a good roper. He could do that stunt he did just now. Rope a steer with the rope around his own neck. He could work in some other stuff. Have you ever done any trick ridin', Dan?'

'Not much.' Dan poised the pen. 'Right here, Mr. Ruffin?'

'Right there.' Ruffin watched Dan sign. 'You'll have to get an outfit. You've got a horse, but you'll need some clothes an' a new saddle. Yore saddle's old an' it won't do.'

'I know that,' Dan returned the pen to the desk. 'I've got some money in the bank. I think it's enough to get what I need.'

'An' you got a hundred comin' from Smokey.' Ruffin folded the contract and chuckled. 'Keep on winnin' bets an' you won't have to take money out of the bank. You go on down to the bunkhouse an' tell Red to show you a bed. You'll want to get yore clothes from home, I guess?'

'I'll ride over after dinner,' Dan stated briefly. 'I can go in to Brule tomorrow an' get the rest of what I need.'

'All right,' Ruffin agreed. 'But don't try to buy show clothes in Brule. They haven't got 'em.' He glanced at his watch. 'Pretty near dinnertime,' he completed. 'I guess that fixes us up.'

Dan recognized dismissal. He said, 'Thanks, Tom,' and started to the door, Carl Thwaite following him.

On the porch Carl said, 'I wish you hadn't done that. I wish you'd let that contract go.'

'It's too late to do any wishin' now,' Dan answered. 'There goes the bell.'

Down at the cookhouse the cook was beating a big iron triangle. Dan went down the steps, and after a moment Carl followed, turning at the bottom to go to the cottage where he and Penny kept house.

There was a good deal of kidding at the dinner table. Red Halsey and Bob White and

18

two or three of the other performers who had wintered with Ruffin had a lot to say. But the talk was rather of what Dan was in for than of what he had done. No reference was made to his break with Bruce, for which Dan was thankful.

After the meal Red Halsey drew Dan aside. 'You'll want yore clothes,' Red said awkwardly. 'If it'll be any accommodation, I'll ride over an' get 'em for you, Dan.'

'Thanks, Red.' Dan looked squarely into Red's friendly eyes. 'But I expect I'd better do that myself. If anybody's goin' to take a cussin', it will be me, an' anyhow I want to see my mother.'

'I *sabe* that.' Red nodded. 'Want me to ride over with you?'

'No, thanks.'

'O.K., Dan. I just thought I'd ask.'

Leaving Red, Dan went down to the pens and, dreading the task before him, asked Buck for a horse.

'Sure,' Buck agreed cheerfully, 'I'll give you Pelican. He needs ridin' anyhow. We just got him in, an' I was wonderin' who I'd get to take his edge off.' Pelican, Dan knew, was fourteen years old and never bucked. A man could do anything on Pelican from carrying cake to falling off under his feet.

'I expect Pelican's just what I need,' he said.

All the way from Ruffin's to the MY, Dan let his imagination run. He was anticipating events, forecasting what was to come. He wished, as he rode, that he had taken Halsey's offer; it would have been easy to let Red do this errand. But he couldn't let Red do the thing he ought to do himself. Reaching the MY, Dan saw Bruce's horse in the corral, still saddled, and mentally braced himself for the meeting with his father.

All his imagination and anticipation were for nothing. Clara was alone in the kitchen when Dan came in and, wordlessly, she put her arms around her son and kissed him.

'I'm goin' with Tom Ruffin, Mother,' Dan said. 'I've come over after my clothes.'

'I know, son,' Clara answered. 'I've got them ready for you. I wish I'd washed yesterday. You've only got two clean shirts.'

Dan could not keep back a smile. 'Two shirts will be plenty,' he assured.

'I packed your things in a suitcase,' Clara announced. 'It's there by the door. You've plenty of handkerchiefs and socks and underwear, and I put in your blue suit. Take it out and hang it up as soon as you can, Dan. You don't want it to get wrinkled.' She was making talk, Dan saw. Her smile was brave, but tears were close behind the smile.

'I'll take care of things, Mother,' Dan said. 'An' I'll write to you. You mustn't worry.'

'I'll not worry,' Clara promised. 'You're a good boy, Dan, and I know you'll not get into any trouble. Can you carry a suitcase on your horse?'

'I borrowed Pelican. I can carry it.' Dan walked to the door and picked up the suitcase. 'I . . . Well, good-by, Mother. Don't you worry now.'

Clara stood beside the door and Dan bent to kiss her. As he straightened, Bruce Mar came into the kitchen. Dan faced his father defiantly. 'I came over for my clothes,' he said.

'Yore mother packed 'em for you,' Bruce drawled tonelessly. 'You've got all you want?'

'I've got my clothes.'

'Then,' Bruce said, 'there's nothin' to keep you.'

Dan was startled. He had expected more than this, had anticipated anger and recrimination. Clara moved back so that Dan stood alone.

'Well, what are you waitin' for?' Bruce stared at his son. 'For me to ask you to come back? I don't want you!'

Still Dan did not move, and in Bruce the dam broke. 'Get out!' he rapped. 'Get off the place. You don't belong here!'

'I'm gettin' out,' Dan said. 'I know I don't belong here. Good-by, Mother.' The door closed behind his broad shoulders.

Pelican offered no objection to the suitcase, but trotted all the way back to Ruffin's with it bumping against his shoulder. The bunkhouse was deserted when Dan came in. He unpacked and hung up the blue suit, then sat down on his

21

bed and stared at the opposite wall until Red Halsey came in.

'I turned Pelican out,' Red announced, sitting down beside Dan. 'You wasn't goin' to use him any more, was you?'

'No. Thanks, Red.'

'Look, kid,' Halsey said. 'There's lots of things for a man to do besides thinkin'. How about yore comin' out an' helpin' me shoe a horse? I got him in, an' he's a damn' wil'cat. He'll kick an' bite an' do anythin' he can think of, an' we'll have a good time cussin' him. Come on.'

'All right,' Dan agreed. 'I'll help you shoe the horse.'

*   *   *

Next morning there was a veritable exodus from Ruffin's ranch. Ruffin was going to Brule to make arrangements for having his cars shifted, Smokey Darnell and Captain Purrington had business in town, and Carl Thwaite, laconically told Dan that he would go in with him. Red Halsey also had business in Brule, as did Bob White, and at the last minute Nevada Warren appeared, ready for the trip. Ruffin had ordered the carryall hitched, and that ample vehicle was loaded to capacity when it creaked away from the ranch toward the little depot at Tejon.

In the smoker of the passenger local Dan

22

and Carl disposed themselves comfortably and watched the others settle into place. Dan had borrowed ten dollars from Ruffin and, after they were seated, counted the change from his ticket. Carl, eying him, said, 'Bein' careful of yore money, kid? It's a good habit. Do you know what an outfit's goin' to cost you?'

Dan shook his head.

'You've got a horse,' Carl drawled. 'That saves you a little, providin' you can use him. You'll have to train him, an' that takes time, so you'll use one of Ruffin's horses at first. Yore saddle will cost you between two an' three hundred dollars. My saddle cost two-fifty. The rest of yore tack—bridles an' such—will put another fifty to a hundred on the bill. You'll need spot cord an' some rope, an' that will be about ten. Then you'll have to have two costumes. The boots will cost you fifty a pair, the pants twenty, the shirts ten, an' you'll spend forty dollars on a hat. Figure it up.'

Dan's eyes narrowed. 'I've got three hundred in the bank,' he said. 'Smokey owes me a hundred an'...'

'Don't count on that. You won't get it. Smokey's always broke.'

'I'll get it or take it out of his hide,' Dan drawled. 'I've got four hundred dollars. I can get an advance from Tom for the rest of it, an' maybe I can buy some secondhand stuff.'

'Maybe,' Carl said skeptically. 'Why were you so hell-bent on goin' with the show, Dan?

You know you'd been better off at the ranch.'

'I've had enough of the ranch to do me,' Dan stated quietly. 'Carl, why did you ask Ruffin where he was goin' to use me?'

Carl shrugged. 'I thought maybe you'd counted on tyin' up with me,' he drawled. 'You might as well find out first as last that it's every man for himself in this business.'

Dan nodded curtly. 'I'll remember that,' he stated.

Tejon was thirty miles from Brule, and the trip by train took a little more than an hour. It was half-past eleven when Brule was reached, and the party separated. Dan, walking uptown with Carl and Red Halsey, said that he was going to the bank. 'I want to get in before noon,' he said. 'They close for dinner.'

'We'll see you down at the Albany then,' Halsey instructed. 'That's where we'll eat.'

Dan experienced some difficulty in withdrawing his account from the Stockman's Bank of Brule. The money had been put on time deposit and its period was not up. He explained his case to Max Fisher, the bank's active vice-president. 'I'm going with Tom Ruffin's show an' I've got to have the money for an outfit. If you don't want to take my word for it, I'll get Tom to talk to you.' Ruffin, president of the bank, could straighten out the difficulty, Dan was sure, and apparently Fisher had the same idea.

'There's no use in bothering Mr. Ruffin,' he

said. 'I'll take care of it for you.'

Dan wrote a check, and Fisher brought the money from the teller's cage. 'Now if you'll just sign this card, Mr. Mar,' he directed, 'I think that will be all.'

As Dan returned card and pen to Fisher he noted that the front door of the bank was closed and the shades drawn. It was the noon hour.

'Thank you, Mr. Mar,' Fisher said. 'I'm sorry that you've closed your account, but I hope you'll do business with us in the future. Will you use the side door when you go out?'

'Sure,' Dan agreed, and started around the end of the counter. As he turned the corner one of the bank employees backed slowly toward him, hands lifted, and behind the bank clerk were three masked men, every one with his hat pulled low and every one carrying a gun in a competent fist. Staring into the unwinking muzzle of a Colt, Dan, too, raised his hands.

'That's right,' a voice rasped from behind the first mask. 'Get 'em up. All of you! This is a holdup!'

Dan was the only customer in the bank, and of the banking force only the clerk who had backed in, a teller, a woman bookkeeper, and Fisher remained. The three armed men were entirely in charge, and they seemed to know exactly what to do.

'Lie down on the floor,' commanded the man who had spoken. 'All of you. You'—he jerked his gun toward Fisher—'take me to the vault!'

It would have been foolhardy to resist. Reluctantly Dan lay down. He heard the leader say, 'You stay here an' watch 'em,' and knew that one bandit had been delegated the task.

Lying face down, Dan heard Fisher's expostulations as he led the way toward the vault. The woman bookkeeper moved, and a voice growled: 'Stay down! Don't turn yore head!'

These men were smart, Dan thought. They were not taking chances on anyone's recognizing them, nor were they giving their victims an opportunity to study them so that later description would be possible. Only Fisher, of all the people in the bank, would have that chance, and Fisher must be busy and too frightened for coherent thinking.

'Now,' a voice rasped, 'get on yore feet an' look straight ahead.' Dan got up and shook his clothes in place. He was careful to keep his hands shoulder high as he moved, for there was a hair-trigger atmosphere about the whole proceeding that warned for caution.

'Get into the vault,' the voice directed.

Dan followed the woman bookkeeper as they entered the vault. Fisher was lying on the floor, bleeding from a gash on his head. The bookkeeper squealed when she saw Fisher, and a bandit growled, 'That's what he got for gettin' funny. He had a gun in the vault.'

'We'll suffocate in here,' the woman pleaded. 'Please don't lock us in the vault.'

'Don't use any air yellin'. You'll be all right.'

Behind Dan there was a scuffle and a squeal. Turning, he saw the little clerk pitch toward him. He caught the small man, lowering him to the floor as the door swung shut. Just as it closed he had a waist-high view of one of the masked men. The door eased soundlessly into place and the bolts clicked, while behind Dan Mar the woman sobbed noisily. The clerk was not unconscious but he bled from a gash across his forehead where a gun sight had cut.

'Stop that!' Dan commanded the sobbing woman sharply. 'We'll be all right. Let's see how bad Fisher's hurt!'

Fisher was badly injured. He had been struck not once but several times, and his breathing was stentorian and shallow. They stretched him out on the floor and did what they could, which was very little.

Dan and his companions remained in the vault for half an hour. At the end of that time the white-faced cashier swung open the door and fresh air rushed in. A good deal of turmoil followed their release. A doctor came, made a quick examination of Fisher, and ordered him taken to Brule's hospital. Art Murrah, Brule County's sheriff, arrived with his deputies and took charge. The doors of the bank were kept closed and the public held out. Tom Ruffin came in and those directors of the bank who

27

lived in town. The little clerk was taken away to have his wound stitched and bandaged, and the cashier, after a hasty examination, announced that between fifteen and twenty thousand dollars had been taken but that he could not give a complete report until after he had made a thorough count. The district attorney arrived, asked questions and more questions, and presently the officers and the witnesses, those who were able, adjourned to the sheriff's office.

CHAPTER THREE

In Murrah's office, with the sheriff and the district attorney again asking questions, the witnesses' statements were reduced to writing. All agreed that three masked men, wearing blue suits and black hats, had robbed the bank. They agreed, too, as to the size of the men. 'There were two about as big as you or me, Mr. Murrah,' Dan said. 'Just average-sized men. An' there was one pretty big fellow. He was about Tom Ruffin's size an' pretty near as heavy as Tom.'

The clerk's pen scratched, and Dan frowned. 'There was something else,' he reported, dipping back into memory. 'One of them wore a kind of watch charm. On a fob, I think. It was a little saddle; you know, like you can buy in a jeweler's.'

'Which one of 'em?' Murrah asked.

Dan shook his head. 'I just had a glimpse of it,' he reported. 'I was down on my knees holdin' the clerk when they closed the vault door, an' that's when I saw it.'

'Was it gold or silver?'

'I don't know.' Dan scowled again. 'All I know is it was a saddle.'

'That's not much to go on,' the attorney said. 'There's been a fad for that kind of thing. Benton's window was full of them a month ago, saddles, spurs, hats, all kinds. I bought one myself.' He displayed a small pair of spurs that dangled from his watch chain. 'You can check on it, Art. Maybe Benton can give you a list of who bought stuff like that.'

Murrah nodded. 'Anything else, Dan?'

'Not a thing.' Dan laughed ruefully. 'I spent most of my time in the bank lyin' on my face.'

'Well . . .' Murrah said. 'I guess you folks can go. Sign your statements first. If any of you think of anything you've missed, you can add it. Yo're goin' to be in town, Dan?'

'There's no train till tomorrow,' Dan said. 'Right here?' This to the clerk. That worthy nodded, and Dan signed his statement. As he finished, Murrah's deputy came into the office.

'We found these in the alley, Art,' he announced. 'They wore 'em in the robbery.' The deputy placed three squares of silk on the desk.

29

Murrah and the district attorney each picked up a piece of silk and Dan took the third. It was a mask, well made, the eyeholes bound and the edges reinforced with tie strings at the top and bottom.

'Looks like they figured on usin' these awhile,' Murrah growled. 'They spent plenty of pains makin' 'em. All right, Dan. You can go.'

Returning the mask to the desk, Dan left the office. Red Halsey and Carl Thwaite were in the corridor waiting for him.

' 'Bout time Murrah turned you loose,' Red complained. 'What did he ask you?'

'Everything I knew an' a lot I didn't,' Dan answered. 'They found the masks those fellows wore.'

'We saw them,' Carl announced. 'The deputy showed 'em to us when he brought 'em in.'

'My belly,' Red complained, 'has got an idea my throat's cut. We got a room at the Albany, Dan. Let's go down there an' clean up.'

Dan was more than agreeable. The three friends left the courthouse and walked to the hotel, Dan between his two fellows, answering questions as they progressed.

At the table in the Albany dining room Dan was the center of a group of interested people, all stopping to ask questions. As he was drinking a final cup of coffee Dan looked up to see Smokey Darnell beside him.

'Well, Mar,' Darnell said, 'I see you didn't get banged up in the bank robbery. You an' the woman seem to be the only ones that didn't.'

Dan caught the implication in Smokey's words. 'Meanin'?' he drawled.

'Meanin' that you kept yore head, Dan,' Carl said quickly.

'Yeah.' Darnell nodded. 'You kept yore head. They say that Fisher is goin' to be all right though. He's talked to Murrah a little. Fisher had a gun in the vault an' he tried for it. You've got to hand it to him—*he* had guts.'

'An' you think I didn't,' Dan drawled.

Smokey Darnell shrugged. 'You sure jump at things,' he answered. 'I didn't say that, did I?'

'No, but...'

'Cut it out, Dan,' Red Halsey rasped. 'Say, Smokey, when are you goin' to pay Dan an' me the bet you lost?'

Darnell produced a roll of bills from his pocket. 'I'll pay you right now,' he stated, counting money. 'Here's yores, Red. Here's a hundred, Mar. I still claim you didn't win the bet. That wasn't trick ropin'.'

Dan did not touch the money that Darnell placed on the table. 'Mebbe you'd like to try again?' he challenged.

Darnell shrugged. 'At trick ropin'? Any time.'

'Then keep it till you think I've won it.'

'An' have you say I welshed the bet? No,

thanks.' Smokey returned the roll to his pocket. 'We'll say you won this bet fair an' square. There'll be another time.' Turning, he swaggered across the dining room.

'Take the money, Dan,' Red Halsey urged. 'You won it, an' if yo're goin' to stay in the show business, Gawd knows you'll need it!'

After they left the dining room Red and Dan sat in the Albany's lobby where again they were the center of a group, Red basking in a sort of reflected glory while Dan told the curious all about the bank robbery. It was ten o'clock before Carl rejoined them and the three went to their rooms.

As Dan undressed, placing his valuables on the dresser, he saw Carl's watch. 'This is what I was tellin' you about,' he announced, picking up the timepiece. 'That fellow had a fob like yours, Carl.' Dan indicated the strap which held the small replica of a saddle at its end.

Carl and Red came to the dresser. 'Like mine?' Carl asked.

'Yeah. He was wearin' a little saddle.'

Carl laughed. 'It couldn't be like this one, Dan,' he said. 'Ruffin gave this to me. It's got my name on the back.' He turned the fob, and Dan saw the neat engraving.

'Carl,' Red said seriously, 'was that what we did in place of playin' pool? Did we go down to the bank an' rob it?'

'We must of.' Carl's face was as serious as Red's. 'That's when you ran the table on me an' I fainted. Remember?'

'Go on!' Dan rasped. 'Quit hurrawin'. I tell you, I did see a saddle watch charm down there.'

Both his companions laughed. 'We won't deny it, kid,' Red agreed. 'Did you tell Murrah?'

'Sure. He didn't seem to think much of it.' Dan picked up the watch again and examined the fob. It was a beautiful piece of craftsmanship, handmade, with silver stirrups on the gold and a good deal of filigree work. 'Murrah's goin' to check with Benton an' see who he sold them to.'

'Better hide that, Carl,' Red warned. 'First thing you know Dan'll have us both in jail. Tom too. You said the big fellow was about Tom's size, didn't you, Dan?'

'By gosh, that's an idea.' Dan replaced the watch on the dresser. 'There's sure to be a reward offered. I'll just go down to Murrah's office in the mornin' and turn you three in. Ruffin an' Carl Thwaite an' Red Halsey, bank robbers. I'll bet that's who did it.'

'Split the reward with us, kid,' Red suggested. 'We'll take the money an' go on a bust when we get to Omaha.' He stretched and yawned. 'If I live that long,' Red completed. 'I got up so early this mornin' I met myself goin' to bed. Tomorrow I'm goin' to sleep till traintime.'

'You'll get up with the rest of us,' Carl

asserted; 'an' I'm an early riser. Good night.'

The local passenger train left Brule for the north at four in the afternoon, and because there was no other train to ride, Red and Dan loafed about the county seat, playing pool, visiting, killing time. Talk concerning the bank robbery was rife, and there persisted a rumor that the bank robbers had been cheated of their spoils. Dan, visiting the sheriff's office, asked concerning the rumor. Murrah's deputy corroborated the report.

'I don't know how it got out,' he said. 'Murrah's sore as a boil about it, but it's so. A lot of that money they stole had just been shipped in, an' the bank had the numbers on the bills. They got a list out, an' anybody that tries to spend that dough is goin' to be surprised. They'll sure get arrested.'

It gave Dan a pleasurable excitement to stay around the sheriff's office, and he was loath to leave. He had never been connected with any crime and, as a witness, he was part of the fever that stirred Brule. But Red had no such interest, and so, having talked awhile longer with the deputy, they left.

At four o'clock the party from Ruffin's were at the depot, and when the train pulled out Dan and Red and Carl were in the smoker.

'Where's Smokey?' Carl asked as the train moved. 'I didn't see him get on.'

'I did.' Red grinned. 'He's back in the chair car with Nevada. Guess he's tryin' his luck with

34

her.'

Carl scowled, and Dan looked inquiringly at Red. 'Smokey thinks he's a ladies' man,' Red explained. 'He won't have much luck with Nevada. *That* gal's hard as nails.'

'But Darnell's married,' Dan expostulated.

'An' that's the hell of it.' Red got up and stretched. 'I think I'll go back an' sit with 'em awhile. I'll bet Smokey will be glad to see me ... *not!*'

The train was sliding along through the yards, and the red sides and yellow lettering of Ruffin's cars crawled past the window. 'Ruffin's Wild West' the lettering read. Dan got a thrill from the words.

'Be ridin' those pretty soon,' he observed.

'Yes, damn it!' Carl's answer was almost vicious. 'I wish we weren't.'

'Why?' Dan was startled by the savagery of the voice.

'Because I do!' After a moment Carl added an amendment. 'I wish I'd never sold the place!'

'Why did you, then?'

'Because'—Carl looked at his seatmate—'I was broke.' He paused momentarily. Then: 'Dad had been sick a long time an' I had to pay the bills. The bank owned most of the place anyhow, but I wish I'd kept it. It would have made a home for Penny.'

'Penny wouldn't stay without you,' Dan observed. 'Anyhow, she likes the show.'

35

'That's the trouble. She likes the show an' everythin' that goes with it.' Carl turned so that he did not look at Dan. 'She's nothin' but a kid, an' she can't see through things.'

The train was out of Brule now and rolling through the brown range country. Carl, as though his talking was finished, settled himself in the seat and tipped his hat down over his nose. 'Look out the window an' see the country,' he drawled. 'You'll get tired of it after a while. Me, I'm goin' to sleep.'

All the party for Ruffin's ranch loaded into the carryall that was waiting when the train reached Tejon. Upon arrival at the ranch the group separated, Nevada and Purrington going to the big house where they had rooms, Carl and Smokey strolling off toward the cottages, and Dan and Red Halsey heading for the bunkhouse. In the bunkhouse the first thing that Dan did was to take his money from his pocket and, sitting on his bed, separate it into two piles.

'Quite a wad,' Red Halsey commented. 'What you goin' to do with it now?'

'Have you got an envelope, Red?' Dan asked by way of answering.

'Yeah.' Red reached up to the shelf above his bunk. 'Here.'

Dan took the envelope. 'This,' he said, 'is the money Darnell handed me. I'm goin' to put it away.' He thrust the smaller pile of bills into the envelope and sealed the flap.

'What's the idea?' Halsey inquired.

'Someday we'll have another bet,' Dan answered. 'If I win it I'll keep that money. If I don't I'll hand him back the same money he gave me.'

'How do you know it's the same money?' Red asked, grinning. 'You've got a wad of it there.'

'He gave me five twenties,' Dan answered. 'They're all new. That's what he gave me, all right.'

The clamor of the cook's triangle interrupted further conversation.

*   *   *

Ruffin returned to the ranch next day and immediately began preparations for leaving. He had ordered his cars delivered to the Tejon siding, and time was short. Concurrent with Ruffin's arrival, Bruce Mar came to the ranch. Dan saw his father riding away just as he came out of the barn to answer Ruffin's summons to the house. Bruce saw his son but made no gesture of recognition.

Ruffin was working at his desk when Dan entered and did not look up for a few minutes. Then, pushing away the letter he was writing and removing his spectacles, he glanced at Dan. 'I wanted to see you,' he said. 'Sit down.'

Dan was apprehensive and seated himself gingerly.

'Bruce was here a minute ago,' Ruffin began without preamble. 'He'd heard about the bank robbery in Brule, an' somebody told him you'd been hurt. He said yore mother was worried.'

Dan said nothing and Ruffin smiled. 'Are you real sure you want to go with me?' he asked. 'We could tear up that contract, you know.'

'I'm real sure,' Dan answered grimly. 'If you don't want me you can tear up the contract, but my part of it sticks.'

Ruffin nodded. 'Then I'll not tear it up,' he said. 'I think you could go back home if you wanted to. I think that Bruce would be all right, but if you don't want to go...'

'I don't want to go.'

'Well'—Ruffin leaned back in his chair—'I didn't get you up here to talk about that. I want to talk about your act. Have you got anything in mind?'

'Nothin' except what you said the other day. About me ropin' the steer an' maybe spinnin' a rope some.'

'I'm afraid that won't be enough. You see, Dan, an act's got to be showy. I know what kind of nerve it takes to rope a steer with the other end of the rope around your neck, but the average customer won't. They're Eastern people an' they won't get it. You'll have to work out somethin' fancy.'

Dan nodded.

'I'll use you ridin' broncs an' ropin' steers

when we start out,' Ruffin continued. 'You don't have to rehearse that. But I wish you had an act. I wish that you could work with Carl an' Penny. You'd fit in there, an' it would help them out too. Why don't you talk to Carl about it?'

'I don't think Carl wants me,' Dan said.

'Ask him.' Ruffin's smile was tolerant. 'Carl didn't want you to sign up; he's down on the show business for some reason. You talk to him, Dan. He's yore friend an' he ought to help you out. That's all I had in mind.'

'I'll talk to Carl,' Dan agreed. 'Thanks, Tom.'

Dan did not find Carl. Penny told him that her brother was out, and Bob White, questioned, said that Carl had gone up to Smokey Darnell's. Dinnertime came and Dan had not seen his friend. There was some talk at dinner concerning the impending departure from the ranch, but there was more talk of the stock that was to go. The show horses were in, but Ruffin carried a bunch of steers for the roping acts and seven buffalo. These were to be gathered that afternoon.

'An' you show hands are goin' to do it,' young Buck Ruffin stated. 'I've got work for my men.'

'Mebbe you think we can't,' Red Halsey gibed. 'Is that yore idea, Buck?'

'I don't know whether you can or not,' Buck answered. 'But if it's done at all, you'll do it.'

When they left the cookshack the men went directly to the corral: Thwaite, Smokey, Captain Purrington, Dan, all the show hands as well as Buck Ruffin's men. Penny came down with her brother, and Red, in the corral roping mounts, called jocularly to her:

'Got to make the women work too. Come on, Penny. Saddle up.'

The whole group left the corrals together. Dan rode beside Carl and Penny, and Red Halsey, taking the lead, proclaimed himself roundup boss.

'It ain't often I get to ramrod a crew,' he announced. 'Them buffalo are in the west pasture, clear to hell an' gone, up by Turkey Mountain. I'm goin' up there after 'em. Carl an' Penny an' Dan will come with me. The steers are closer home. I'll set the circles.'

There was a good deal of laughter and jest among the riders, but Red was as good as his word. He dropped riders off in pairs, as any roundup boss would do, Darnell and Purrington the last. Then, with the Thwaites and Dan, Red struck north toward Turkey Mountain.

'You an' Penny take the west side, Carl,' he ordered. 'Dan an' me'll lope around the east end.'

'I want to talk to Carl,' Dan objected.

'Then I'll take the east side,' Red answered. 'They ain't there anyhow. You folks will find 'em.'

'Carl,' Dan said when Red was gone, 'I talked to Tom this mornin' an' he said that he thought I'd fit into your act. How about it?'

Carl Thwaite hesitated for an instant. 'I don't think so,' he answered slowly. 'Maybe you would, but I think there ought to be one man roper in an act. Penny an' I have practiced a long time, an' we've got our act set.'

'I told him you didn't want me.' Dan's disappointment showed on his face. 'That's that, then.'

'It ain't that I don't want you,' Carl said. 'It's ... Dan, yore dad was over this mornin'. I had a little talk with him. Why don't you go home? That's where you belong.'

Dan's face hardened. 'You don't want me with the show,' he charged. 'You know I won't go home.'

'Why won't you?' Carl demanded. 'There's not any reason. The trouble with you is that you don't try to get along with yore dad. Everything he's got he's built for you. Everything he does is on yore account. Maybe he is hard on you—I don't know about that— but I do know that he's broke just in the last few days since you've been gone. It's turned him into an old man. Ruffin would let you off. I talked to him an' he said he would.'

Dan shook his head. 'I'll not go back,' he stated. 'I'm done at the MY.'

'Then all I can say is that yo're a hardheaded young fool!' Carl rasped. Both men had forgotten Penny. 'Here you've got a chance to...'

'To go home an' be bossed around! Seems to me you've paid a lot of attention to my business.'

'Somebody ought to pay attention to it. You won't!'

Dan's eyes glittered behind their narrowed lids. 'I wonder why you've bothered so much,' he drawled. 'First you go to Ruffin an' get him to let me off my contract, an' then you talk to Bruce an' get him to say I can come back if I'll be a good little boy. You don't want me in yore act, either. It wouldn't be because you can't stand competition, would it? Maybe yo're afraid I'll show you up like I did Darnell!'

No man relishes a thing like that, and Carl Thwaite was proud of his roping. 'You swelled-headed pup,' he snapped. 'Afraid of you showin' me up? I'll say not! I can lick you at anythin' you say, any time.'

'Crawl down off that horse,' Dan invited. 'We'll see if you can lick me.'

Carl freed a foot from the stirrup. Dan was already on the ground. Penny, face white, rode between them. 'You'll not fight!' she commanded. 'You won't!'

Carl dropped back into his saddle, and Dan, his face showing his shame, turned his horse. 'I guess I lost my head,' he muttered. 'I'm sorry, Penny.'

'Dan,' Carl said, 'we're a pair of fools. I got

42

sore. I ... Come on back an' we'll talk it over.'

Dan did not turn his head. He rode steadily toward the shoulder of Turkey Mountain and, as brother and sister watched him, stirred his horse to a long lope.

'He'll be all right,' Carl said. 'I'll talk to him when we get in an' maybe work out a way to fit him into the act. Let's go around this side, Penny.'

*   *   *

Dan found Red Halsey well toward the north end of Turkey Mountain with the seven buffalo and plenty of trouble.

'I'm damned glad you got here,' Red vouchsafed as Dan rode up. 'These things are harder to drive than a covered wagon, an' just about as slow. Where's Carl an' Penny?'

'I left 'em comin' around the other side.'

'Get yore talkin' done?'

'Yeah.' Dan nodded and took down his rope. 'Maybe we can shake these buffalo up a little.'

'A rope don't do no good,' Halsey informed gloomily. 'They don't feel it no more than a tick bite. Hi-yuh! Git along! Damn yore black hides, you ...!'

It was slow work driving the buffalo. The animals paid no attention whatever to yells, and scarcely more to ropes dragged off their rumps. They were docile enough and used to

43

being driven, but when they were crowded too closely they turned, lowered their heads, and prepared to charge.

'I wish Carl an' Penny would show up,' Dan said as they brought their charges to the end of the mountain. 'They'd be a help.'

'I think they seen us an' went home,' Red replied. 'Carl's drove these things before, an' he ain't no fool.'

The sun was down when Red and Dan brought their drive to the pens at headquarters. There were many and sundry gibes thrown at them as they pushed the buffalo through the corral gate. The buffalo unconcernedly began to eat hay, and Red and Dan, dismounting, answered the kidding.

'Where's Carl an' Penny?' Red demanded. 'They was supposed to help. Wait till I see Carl. What won't I tell him!'

'They aren't in yet,' Bob White answered. 'Say ...' He glanced at the sun, touching the rim of the horizon.

Instant alarm filled the faces about Dan and Red. 'You don't suppose somethin's happened, do you?' Bob White said.

'We'll go an' see,' Red snapped. 'Whereabouts did you leave 'em, Dan?'

'On the east side of Turkey Mountain.' Dan was already in his saddle. 'They were all right.'

'Likely we'll find 'em ridin' in,' Red said. 'There's no need to worry. They ... What's that yonder? Goin' into the draw?'

44

Every eye was turned toward the long draw that quartered the pasture beyond the fence. A horse came out of the draw.

'Carl's horse!' Red snapped. 'Come on!'

Reaching the horse, they caught it, and as Dan held the animal's reins Red looked at the saddle and shook his head.

'Spur tracks across the seat,' he reported. 'Carl's been throwed.'

Smokey Darnell's voice was shrill. 'There's blood on this side, on the jockey.'

'Bob,' Red ordered, 'you take the horse in an' tell Ruffin. We're goin' out.'

The sun was fully down by the time the little posse reached Turkey Mountain.

'This is where I left 'em,' Dan said, halting. 'Right here.'

Red lifted his voice in a long yell, the eerie wail that only a cowpuncher can use without cracking vocal cords. 'Penneeee! Whooooo! Penneeee! Carl! Oh, Carl!'

They waited while the echoes died away along the mountainside.

'Penneeee! Carl! Oh, Carl!'

'Wait a minute, Red. I think I hear somethin' up ahead.' Every man listened. Was it a shout or the echo of Red's yell they had heard?

'That's her!' Dan snapped. 'Come on.'

Red called again as they rode, and now, listening, they could hear the unmistakable answer. 'Up the draw,' Red said and, turning, led the way.

At the top of the draw they found their quarry. Penny came slowly toward them on foot, and behind Penny something lay on the ground, long and quiet in the fading light.

'Carl.' Penny's voice held no inflection; terrifying it was, for all the emotion had been drained from it. 'He's up there.'

Red dropped down from his horse and the others rode on slowly. 'He thought he saw the buffalo,' Penny's dreadful, toneless voice went on. 'He told me to wait. When he didn't come back I followed him. I found him ... like that!'

Dismounting, the men stood about what had been Carl Thwaite. The man lay on his back, face upturned to the sky where now stars were appearing. Buck Ruffin's voice was filled with awe. 'His horse got him. See where he was dragged?'

Dan Mar, lifting his eyes from the dead man, looked at Penny. Her face was a small white flower in the dusk.

'If you'd stayed, Dan, it wouldn't have happened,' she said, still in that dreadful, level voice. 'You'd have been with him. It wouldn't have happened.'

CHAPTER FOUR

Memory swings a bullhide whip. In Tom Ruffin's car Dan felt the lash as lividly and

46

truly as though Penny used it on his back. Ruffin, at his desk, looked over his steel-framed spectacles, first at the girl and then at Dan. Penny had just arrived and was still in her traveling costume.

'I been talkin' to Penny,' Ruffin announced. 'I had the idea that the two of you could get together an' give me another rope act. She says not.'

Dan made no reply, and Ruffin fingered the papers on his desk. 'I had that idea all along,' he continued. 'Ever since Penny told me that she'd join us. Seems like it won't work. I wish you two would talk it over.' He arose ponderously. 'I'll be back in a minute.'

With Ruffin gone, Dan looked at Penny and the girl returned his scrutiny. It was Penny who broke the awkward silence. 'Tom wants us to do an act together. I just can't, Dan.'

'I expect I'd feel the same way,' Dan said slowly. 'I know you blame me.'

Penny flushed delicately. 'No, Dan,' she corrected, 'I was out of my head when I said that. I'd been with Carl, and when I found him I ... Well, I had to blame someone. I've thought about it a lot. I wasn't fair to you. Even if you'd been there, you couldn't have kept Carl's horse from falling.'

'You're tryin' to let me off easy.' Dan kept his eyes steadily on the car floor. 'You haven't blamed me any more than I've blamed myself. It's all right, Penny. You're goin' along with

47

the show?'

'Yes. There's nothing else I can do. I have to live.'

'I wish,' Dan said, 'that there was somethin' I could do. If you want to go back to Brule an' stay, I'll see that you've got money enough to do it. I ...'

'Thank you, Dan, but I couldn't do that.' Penny smiled wanly. 'I'm going with the show.'

Coming back into the office, Ruffin saw at a glance that there had been no agreement between these two young people. 'Well, Penny,' he said briskly, 'what do you plan to do?'

'Smokey wrote to me,' Penny replied. 'He and Belle can use me in their act. I'm going with him.'

Ruffin nodded. The arrangement was good, although he would have been better pleased had Dan and Penny combined. 'That's between you an' Smokey,' he said. 'He's already usin' one of yore horses. He said you'd written him he could.'

'I did.' Penny turned to business with relief. 'About the tack, Mr. Ruffin. I'll use my own, of course, but you brought Carl's saddle and all the rest, didn't you?'

'I brought it along.'

'I need the money, Mr. Ruffin,' Penny said. 'Do you think you could sell it for me?'

Ruffin nodded. 'You'll have to tell me what you want for it.'

'I made a list.' Penny fumbled in her small handbag. 'Here.'

Ruffin glanced at the list. 'Maybe you'll have to take payments,' he warned, 'but I think I can sell it all right.'

'And now I think I'll go to the car.' Penny got up. 'The drayman is bringing my trunk down from the depot. I'm going to live with Ruth?'

'Just like you always have,' Ruffin replied heartily. 'I put Ruth alone so that you'd have a place when you got here. Take it easy for a day or so, Penny. Don't try to work till you've rehearsed awhile.'

'Thank you.' Penny smiled. 'Smokey said that we'd rehearse before I worked in the act.' Nodding to Dan, she left the car, and Ruffin went back to his desk.

'Well,' he said, 'that's that. I'd hoped that you an' Penny could get together; I need another rope act, an' that's a fact. Guess I'll have to write an' see if I can get one.' Sitting down, the big man picked up a paper from the desk. Dan knew that he was dismissed but he did not leave at once.

'About Carl's tack,' he began abruptly. 'I'd like to buy it.'

Ruffin looked up. 'Yeah?' he said. 'I guess you could use it. Carl's saddle would be O.K. for you.'

'I want to buy it all.'

'You'll have no use for a lot of it,' Ruffin

49

warned.

'I want it all,' Dan said firmly. 'I can put a hundred down on it, an' I'd like to have you take the rest out of my pay.'

'I can do that,' Ruffin agreed. 'I'll tell Brannigan to put the chest in the pad room, an' I'll get the key from Penny. Anythin' else, Dan?'

'Not right now.' Dan turned to go.

Ruffin, something of a rough-and-ready psychologist, called him back. 'Dan.'

'Yeah?'

'Don't you go around blamin' yoreself for what happened to Carl. There's other men been killed because a horse fell with 'em. It was tough luck an' all that, but it happened an' it can't be helped. You weren't any more to blame than I was.'

'Thanks, Tom.'

'An' another thing: Yo're a good trick roper, an' I need a rope act. Get yoreself a pardner. Ruth is workin' single. Talk to her about tyin' up with you. I pay an act more than I do one performer, an' you two might work out somethin'. Get busy on it!'

'Thanks, Tom,' Dan said again.

'All right. Now get yore head up an' get out of here. I'm busy.'

Leaving Ruffin's car, Dan walked toward the lot. The show had pulled into Des Moines at midnight, but already the big rag was up, the sun shining from its new white canvas. The cookhouse, pad room, and stock tent were in place, and the rhythmical ringing of mauls on iron stakes, and the 'Heave ... yo! Heave ... yo!' of the boss canvasman spoke of other tops in the process of erection. Beside the big top the tepees of the Sioux who traveled with the show flaunted their painted cones. Three loads of hay were going into the stock tent under the anxious supervision of the boss hostler, and two grocery carts stood beside the cookhouse. The whole lot seethed with movement of performers, roustabouts, hostlers; and curious townspeople—small boys and men, 'lot lice,' the show people called them—stood around or got in the way, as nature moved them. For a month Dan Mar had been a part of this movement and color.

Red Halsey was in the pad room fitting a new cinch to his saddle when Dan arrived. 'Well?' Halsey questioned his friend.

Dan shook his head. 'She's goin' to work with Smokey,' he said. 'She still blames me for Carl bein' killed.'

Red scowled. 'Yo're no more to blame than me. I took Carl up there.'

Dan sat down beside Red. 'Mebbe not,' he said. 'She figures different. I do too ... I bought Carl's tack.'

Red's eyes were sharp. 'She want to sell it?'

Dan nodded. Red pursed his lips in a small, soundless whistle. 'You don't need it if you aren't goin' to do a rope act. It'll cost you plenty. How much?'

'I didn't ask.'

Again the soundless whistle.

'Tom told me that he'd use a rope act if I could get a pardner. He said I might team up with Ruth Shattuck.'

'You goin' to try?'

Dan shook his head. Red, picking up the cinch, twisted it straight. 'Well,' he drawled, 'if I could spin a rope good I'd throw in with you.'

Dan laughed. Red Halsey trying to spin a rope and dance through it would be a good deal like a bear standing on its head. He'd get the job done but it would be funny. Red was a bulldogger par excellence and a bronc rider able to compete with any man, but he was no trick roper.

'Funny, ain't it?' Red said shortly.

'You'll do to take along, Red.' Dan put his hand on his friend's shoulder. 'You sure stay with a man.'

'I aim to,' Red returned, mollified.

Nevada Warren came up to the pad room leading Gold, her palomino trick horse. The girl nodded to Red and Dan and with deft hands began to saddle Gold.

'Hey, Nevada,' Red said, 'there ain't no parade in Des Moines. It's too big a town.'

'I know it.' Nevada pulled up her latigo. Slight as she was, she allowed no one else to saddle Gold, and rumor had it that only under protest would she let a hostler groom the big yellow horse. Saddle in place, Nevada mounted. Gold looked inquiringly at his mistress and then trotted toward the big top.

'She don't,' Red drawled, 'think any more of that horse than she does of her right eye. It's a wonder she don't sleep in the stock tent with him.'

'He's a good horse,' Dan answered, glad of the change of subject.

'An' she puts on a good show,' Red agreed. 'But she sure stands a man off. Won't have nothin' to do with anybody, unless it's Tom Ruffin. I run into her downtown in Omaha an' asked her to ride back to the lot with me. She says "no, thanks" just as cool as a cucumber. Mebbe I wasn't good enough to ride with her.'

Dan laughed. 'She's standoffish, all right,' he admitted.

'I guess,' Red said, 'that cinch will hold now. I'm goin' to ride that Rocker horse, an' he ain't been with the show long enough to know it's just an act. He really tries to throw you. Let's go uptown an' give the burg the once-over. We got time.'

*   *   *

Ruffin's Wild West played to capacity houses for the first two performances in Des Moines. Tom Ruffin gave the crowds their money's worth, act following act with clocklike precision. Ruffin's Wild West, according to the four sheets, packed 'five hours of entertainment into two and one half hours.' Only two acts worked alone under the big top: Nevada Warren and her trick horse, Gold; and Captain Purrington's shooting exhibition. These, coupled with the spectacles—the 'specs,' the show people called them—were principal features. Ruffin used two spectacles, one a stage holdup and the other an Indian attack on a covered wagon.

Ruffin carried seventy people, not counting Indians, and every performer had a regular place in the show, most of them appearing in more than one act. Dan, for example, rode bucking horses and took part in the steer roping. He was also one of the gallant cowboys who rescued the emigrant family. Red Halsey rode bucking horses, bulldogged, and was one of the bandits who held up the stagecoach in the robbery sequence. Captain Purrington, besides doing his shooting act, served as the leader of the sheriff's posse which captured the stage robbers; and Smokey Darnell, with Belle and Penny, were stage passengers, in addition to the rope act which they staged on the track.

Between the afternoon and evening performances Carl Thwaite's chest was brought down to the pad room and the pad-room boss handed Dan the key. 'Ruffin said to give you this. Where do you want the chest?'

Dan indicated the proper location and when the chest was placed opened it. Carl's saddle, three bridles, various ropes, a pair of chaps, and other appurtenances were in the chest, and one by one Dan removed them. As he worked, rearranging his newly acquired property, he thought of Carl. These were Carl's spurs; this was his saddle, the very saddle he had ridden on the day he died. Dan's finger traced the spur tracks across the seat. These were Carl's ropes. Dan could remember when Carl bought this bit. Memory came back to him, harsh and poignant. He looked up to find Penny standing beside him and hastily closed the lid of the chest.

'I'm glad that you have them, Dan,' Penny said. 'I think ... when you rode off that day, Carl was sorry for what he'd said. He told me that we'd talk when we got back to the ranch and that he thought he could fit you into the act. I wish you'd take them, Dan. I'd like to give Carl's things to you.'

Dan shook his head. 'I can't, Penny. I've made arrangements to buy them, but I can't take them as a present.'

Penny hesitated an instant. The contents of the chest had brought recollection to her, and tears were close. Dan locked the chest. 'You need the money,' he said gently. 'Don't try to give me Carl's things. Come on. I'll walk down to the car with you.'

Penny made no objection, and together the two silently crossed the lot. When they reached the car where Penny roomed with Ruth

Shattuck the girl spoke. 'Wait for me, Dan. There's something I want to give you.'

Dan stood outside while Penny mounted the steps of the car. 'This was Carl's,' she said when she returned. 'I want you to keep it.'

Dan took the small gold saddle still warm from her hand. There was nothing he could say.

'And you must forgive me for what I said.' Penny would not meet Dan's eyes. 'I didn't mean it. I was out of my mind. Please, Dan.'

'Sure, Penny. I'll forget it.'

Penny smiled wanly. 'Thank you, Dan,' she said, and went back into the car.

*   *   *

The next morning in the deserted pad room Dan again opened his chest. There was something he had been wanting to do ever since he acquired the property, and, selecting a length of spot cord and a maguey rope, he went to the arena.

Like the lot, the arena was deserted. Dan looked furtively about and then, sure that he was alone, fell to spinning his rope. He was clumsy at first from lack of practice, but, warming gradually, he made the rope sing. He built a loop and, rolling it, skipped back and forth, working along the arena. Stopping, breathless, he heard a patter of applause and, turning, saw Nevada and Gold at the tent entrance. Flushed with exercise and because he had been discovered, Dan walked back toward the girl.

'That's a good stunt,' Nevada praised frankly. 'I've seen it before, but you're good at it.'

'Thanks.' Dan coiled the rope.

Nevada said: 'You could put on a rope act that would beat Smokey's. Why don't you?'

'I need horses and a pardner,' Dan answered. 'I don't know. Smokey's pretty good.'

'*He* thinks!' Nevada commented pointedly. 'Go get your horse. I'm going to exercise Gold, and then I'll ride some for you.'

Dan shook his head. 'Not on Domino,' he answered. 'I've never roped at him.'

'Go get him!' Nevada ordered, and laughed. 'Do you think I can't handle that hammerheaded appaloosa?'

Dan wanted to rope at a horse, and Nevada was sure and confident. 'All right,' he agreed.

When he returned with Domino, Nevada dismounted from her palomino and stood by while Dan changed her saddle. Domino was a scary horse, full of snort and harmless eye-rolling, and he always swelled when he was saddled. Domino was enough to frighten many a man, but Nevada, grinning, reached for the reins.

'Let me ride him first,' Dan suggested. 'He won't buck, but he's mighty spooky when you first saddle him.'

'Give me that horse,' Nevada commanded disdainfully. 'You've got a half-breed bit on him that would tear his jaw off. Give him here.'

Reluctantly Dan passed over the reins. Nevada led Domino around a narrow circle, put a rein over his neck, and went up before Domino knew what was happening. She rode the horse to the barrier, worked him back and forth, and then called to Dan.

'Drop a rope over his neck. Don't catch him; just drop it over.'

Dan tossed his rope across Domino's sweating white neck. Disliking the rope, Domino fretted and shied and threatened, and Nevada, sitting her saddle as though she were a part of it, talked to the horse. Domino rolled his eyes and, cocking his ears, paced forward, the rope sliding from his neck.

They worked the horse for half an hour, each interested, each intent on what they were doing. At the end of that time Domino, caught by the neck, stopped on his hind feet, sliding to a halt just as though he had worked in a roping act all his life.

Nevada got down. 'He's got sense,' she praised, 'but he sure puts on a show. You could teach him to work in a week. In a month he'd be lying down and rolling over.'

'You sure *sabe* horses,' Dan complimented admiringly. 'There's a lot of boys afraid of Domino. Ruffin wanted to use him for a buckin' horse. He'll buck if you pitch him slack.'

'That's the way to ruin a horse.' Nevada possessed herself of Gold's bridle reins. 'Don't you let Tom have him. That horse will make a good rope horse. All he needs is a little work.' Still talking about Domino, Nevada and Dan went to the pad room. When they separated Nevada made a suggestion.

'Bring him around tomorrow at the same time. We'll give him another workout.' Dan looked his astonishment. This was Nevada Warren, a star, a feature of the show and with a reputation for being high-hat.

Nevada laughed shortly. 'Bring him around an' I'll be there. I like horses.'

'All right,' Dan accepted eagerly. 'I'll do it.'

Ruffin's Wild West played another day in Des Moines before moving on to Davenport. Nevada, good as her word, appeared the following morning, and Dan was there with Domino. It became a habit. In Cedar Rapids Domino felt a rope around his forelegs and stopped, nostrils dilated as he snorted. In Davenport he did not even snort. At Clinton he was placid enough for all purposes when Dan roped his hind legs, and in Peoria Dan caught front feet, hind feet, head, and forelegs, anything he wanted.

'That horse is ready,' he announced as Nevada smiled down at him. 'I'm sure obliged.'

Nevada slapped Domino's sweating neck.

'He's not exactly gentle,' she commented, 'but he'll do. I wish you had another like him for us to work on.'

'So do I,' Dan agreed, and then, ruefully: 'Not that it would do me any good. I need a pardner for a rope act.'

'You might get one,' Nevada said. 'Want to work the horse tomorrow?'

'If you do.'

'I'll be here,' Nevada promised.

Nevada was late in coming to the tent the next morning, and while he waited Dan read a newspaper. A headline blazoned across its top: 'Daring Midnight Robbery. Express Agent Attacked.'

With little interest Dan read the account that followed. At about one o'clock the express office at the depot had been entered by three masked men who held up the night clerk and his helper at gun point. The helper offered resistance and was slugged, and the clerk, forced to open the safe, was tied and gagged.

'No report of the loss has been made public,' the account continued, 'but it is known that a large sum of currency was expected to arrive in town, and the daring bandits may have been well repaid for their work. Police report that every effort is being made to apprehend the criminals, and have several clues. An arrest is expected shortly.'

'Waiting for me?' Nevada asked. 'Sorry I'm late.'

'Just readin' the paper,' Dan answered.

The show moved from Peoria that night, a short jump. By midmorning the tops were up on the lot at the new stand, and at noon there was a parade. During the afternoon show the crowd was boisterous and a little unruly.

'There was a carny through ahead of us,' Red explained when Dan mentioned the actions of the audience. 'I guess it was a griftin' outfit. I heard that there was some trouble fixin' the city council so that we could show at all.'

'Why do we show here after a carnival?' Dan asked.

Red shrugged. 'A mix-up in the routin', likely. Ruffin don't like it. I heard him talkin'.'

During the night performance Dan met Ruth Shattuck in the entry. The girl's face was white beneath her rouge and her eyes were livid with anger. 'That crowd!' Ruth snapped. 'Look at my new blouse!'

A discolored spot soiled the silk squarely in the center of Ruth's back. 'They're throwing stuff. Somebody hit me with an orange just when I did a handstand. Ruffin's got the cops watching, but that won't help. Somebody will get killed in there!' Ruth went on.

Dan, at the tunnel entrance, looked narrow-eyed at the arena. Nevada and Gold were in the ring, and Nevada was having trouble with the big horse. She was white beneath her make-up but masterly and cool, and Dan felt a thrill of pride for the girl. She was certainly a horseman! Dan saw a blue-clad policeman climb into the seats and speak to a group of young men and boys who sat together. Nevada mounted Gold to ride him off. The band struck up a cakewalk and Gold responded. Just at the entrance Nevada turned the horse and made him rear as she always did. Dan ducked back to get out of Gold's way, heard a scream, and jumped forward in time to see Gold come crashing over on his back. Nevada, thrown clear, scrambled up and ran to the horse, and Dan flung himself on the weaving, threshing head to hold Gold quiet. An arena attendant was climbing into the seats and a police whistle shrilled. The arena man yelled, 'Hey, Rube!' and pandemonium filled the tent.

Dan did not heed the tumult. The show's veterinarian came running and knelt beside the horse. His examination was swift, and he straightened, looking into Nevada's panic-stricken eyes. 'Have to move him!' the vet snapped.

Disregarding the bedlam, Dan, Red Halsey, and half a dozen more got Gold on a sled and hauled him out of the big top. In the back yard, with the fight boiling around them, the veterinarian bent again. This time when he straightened he shook his head. 'I'm sorry, Nevada,' the vet said.

'I heard his leg snap when he went down.' Nevada's voice was small in the tumult. 'You can't ...'

The vet shook his head. 'You go away, Nevada,' he ordered.

'No!' Nevada Warren's voice was fierce. 'I'll do it. Get me a gun!'

She stood there, a slight, slim figure, clothed in tragedy. About her lights flared and the fight raged. Little crowds of showmen, acting as units, wielding tent stakes, sticks, whatever they could lay hands on, were driving into the townspeople. A patrol wagon's gong clanged, and there came the shrill, insistent shriek of a police whistle.

'Better let me,' the veterinarian began, and then, seeing Nevada's eyes, stopped. Captain Purrington, tall, gray, silent as always, slid a gun from his holster and held it out. Nevada took the heavy weapon, made a step toward Gold, and brushed her hand across her eyes.

'I can't,' she said, 'I can't,' and collapsed. Dan caught the girl as she fell, a pitifully light, pitifully slender body. He took the big gun from her hand, and his voice was gentle.

'I'll look after him, Nevada.'

The girl looked into Dan Mar's face. Something she saw must have reassured her. 'You, Dan,' she said. 'No one else. You'll look after him?'

'I'll 'tend to it, Nevada. No one else.'

Ruth Shattuck and Penny Thwaite, with some of the other women of the show, were among the performers crowded around. Dan placed Nevada's feet on the ground and spoke to Penny. 'Look after her, Penny. Get her away.'

Penny and Ruth, closing in on either side of the girl, led her away, and Dan turned to the horse. Gold looked at him with liquid, pain-filled eyes, and carefully Dan placed the muzzle of the gun close to a silken ear. The gun jerked sharply in his hand; Gold's feet threshed an instant, and then the horse was still save for the quivering muscles in his upturned hip.

Ruffin, pushing through the crowd, growled an oath. 'A damned drunk shot the horse. Hit him with a twenty-two pistol. A five-thousand-dollar horse destroyed because of a drunken fool. By God, this town will pay for this!'

The fight was dying down. Occasionally some showman bellowed: 'Hey Rube! this way! Hey, Rube!' and men ran past in the darkness. The police whistle had ceased its shrilling.

'An' that,' Dan Mar said, looking at Ruffin, 'won't bring Gold back.'

*　　　*　　　*

On the afternoon of the following day Dan sat in the car watching Illinois cornfields roll past. Across the aisle Red Halsey wore a gorgeous black eye and nursed a pair of skinned knuckles. Red, hunting vengeance, had found it. Ruffin's Wild West was intact albeit somewhat battered. Up in the roustabouts'

64

cars there were plenty of bandaged heads and bruised bodies, but there was exhilaration, too, and much talk. 'You seen that townie go down when I hit him? I bent a tent stake over his head an' he went out like a lamp.' 'We had a bunch of 'em crowded up against the big rag. They couldn't get away.' 'The damned coppers! If they hadn't butted in . . .'

Back in the office car Tom Ruffin, with Fred Kerr his bookkeeper, and with the head canvasman, the chief hostler, and various others, took account of the damage. The fight had been a costly thing; a five-thousand-dollar horse, torn canvas, damaged properties. Ruffin swore.

'The bastards! Do you know how much I paid in fines? Four hundred dollars!'

Dan took no account of all this. He turned from the window and saw Penny Thwaite standing beside his seat.

'Nevada wants you,' Penny said briefly.

Dan followed the girl toward the rear of the train.

Nevada's compartment was at the far end of the married couples' car. As Dan arrived Ruth Shattuck came out.

'Go on in,' she ordered briefly.

There were curtains at the compartment's windows and a matching spread on the bed. On a wall, swaying gently with the movement of the car, hung a picture of a man and woman, both dressed in tights.

Nevada looked at Dan.

'I took care of it, Nevada,' Dan said swiftly. 'I didn't hurt him an' I had him buried.'

He waited. Nevada made a little gesture toward the bed. 'Sit down,' she said.

Awkwardly Dan seated himself. Nevada twisted a ring around and around on her finger. 'Thank you,' she said suddenly.

'That's all right, Nevada.'

Silence again. Nevada looked up. 'Tom wants a rope act,' she said. 'You haven't got a partner and I've lost mine. Maybe we can work together.'

'If you want it that way,' Dan answered quietly. 'We'll try, Nevada.'

CHAPTER FIVE

A new act does not go into performance without hours of rehearsal. Nevada Warren and Dan Mar began with an advantage, for they had already worked together while training Domino. Tom Ruffin, when he heard of the proposed partnership, nodded and announced that it might work out, but later, finding Nevada alone, put some questions.

'Why are you takin' Dan for a pardner? You've always worked single, Nevada.'

Nevada shrugged. 'He hasn't a partner and I've lost Gold. Why not?'

'Look, Nevada,' Ruffin said awkwardly, 'if you need money to buy a new horse an' carry you while you train him, I reckon I could let you have it. I feel like hell about Gold bein' killed. Why don't you draw on me for what you need an' get another horse?'

'That's nice of you, Tom'—Nevada shook her head—'but I don't want to train another horse. Not right now. I couldn't find another one like Gold. I'll work out an act with Dan.'

Ruffin cleared his throat. 'You don't have to work at all if you don't want to,' he reminded. 'You know that.'

Nevada smiled at the big showman. 'We talked about that at the ranch last winter, Tom,' she said gently. 'It wouldn't do. I like you a lot, but...'

'Yeah.' Ruffin nodded. 'Well, Nevada, you do what you want to. You always have.'

'Dan and I will have something to show you in a couple of weeks,' Nevada promised. 'We'll have the act roughed out by then. Thanks a lot, Tom.'

For the first few days after the formation of the partnership there was much consultation while the act was roughed out. Dan came to Nevada's compartment where they could talk alone, leaving the compartment door open as a sop to convention. The conferences were not all business. Nevada, without appearing to pry, learned a good deal about her partner, what he had done, what he hoped to do. Dan held no subterfuge. He was an easy to read as an open book.

'Someday,' he said, 'I'll have an outfit of my own. I'm goin' to raise registered cattle. There's money in it an' they're sure pretty.'

The train was rolling along as they talked, and Dan, glancing out of the car window, lifted his hand to point to a white farmhouse beset with barns.

'There's a fellow that's got what he wants: a good place, a family, neighbors, good stock. Look at those shorthorns!'

A little bunch of red and roan cattle appeared momentarily outside the window.

'You'd like to have a farm?'

Dan laughed. 'Not a farm; a cow ranch. All the farmin' I want to do is to cut enough hay to go through the winter, an' I'll hire somebody to do that. What I want is a bunch of registered Herefords an' a few stock cattle so that I'll have a crop of calves to sell. I'll sell the bull calves from the registered bunch an' keep working until I get all my stuff thoroughbred. Then I'll have the world by the tail with a downhill drag. The ranchmen have got to improve their cattle or these feeders back here won't buy 'em, an' I plan to be right up among the first.'

'You talk as though you were already in the business,' Nevada laughed.

It was hot in the car, but the girl looked as cool and fresh as though she had just come from making her toilet. Dan mopped his

68

forehead.

'How do you do it, Nevada?' he demanded. 'You look like you'd just stepped out of a bandbox. It's hot as tophet in here.'

'I'm used to it,' Nevada answered briefly. 'I've traveled with a show ever since I can remember.'

Dan eyed his companion curiously. 'Seems to me,' he said ruefully, 'I've talked a lot about myself. How about you?'

'About me?'

'Yeah. How do you come to be with Ruffin's show?'

'I told you.' Nevada seemed a little cross. 'I've been with a show all my life. My folks were equestrians. I was born in a wardrobe trunk.'

Dan glanced at the picture of the man and woman in tights. 'Your people?' he asked.

Nevada nodded. 'Father and Mother. They're both dead.'

A moment's silence. 'That's tough,' Dan sympathized.

'It's not so bad. They died doing what they wanted to do. Dad was killed in the ring. He did a triple somersault in the act and his horse shied. The ring edge caught him when he fell. Mother and I did an act for a while, and then she was hurt in a train wreck. She never got well.'

'An' you stuck to the show business.'

The girl shrugged slim shoulders. 'Why not?

69

I was raised in it.'

'Are you always goin' to stay with it?'

Nevada's eyes strayed toward the window. 'Sometimes I think I'd like a home,' she answered. 'I think I'd like a place that was mine, a nice big kitchen with a polished stove and a lot of dishes and a big front room where I could sit down to sew. I'd like to just sit there and look out of the window and see the same country every day. I think maybe that would be heaven.'

The train jerked and slowed, jerked again and came to a groaning stop. As the noise of its progress died, a voice, shrill and filled with venom, came from the corridor. '... I'm not going to have her in the act. I tell you, I won't!'

The Darnells occupied the next compartment, and it was Belle's voice they heard. Nevada made a small grimace, and Dan, rising, went to the door.

'It's always some girl!' Belle shrilled. 'Last year it was Ruth Shattuck and this season it's Penny Thwaite! I know why Carl came to see you that day! He wanted you to keep away from Penny. That's why he wouldn't talk in front of me. Someday I'm going to tell what I know, Smokey Darnell, and when I do ...' Dan closed the door, muffling the voice.

'They're at it all the time,' Nevada said. 'It's things like that that make a girl wonder about getting married.'

'I expect I'd better go,' Dan announced,

glancing at the closed door. 'There's a lot of gossips with this outfit an'...'

Nevada laughed. 'Sit down,' she commanded. 'They can't say anything about me they haven't already said.'

The train started with a series of jerks, and Dan listened to Nevada as she continued to talk. His mind was not on what she said, and after a time the girl, realizing his abstraction, let her voice die away.

'I'd better go,' Dan announced and, rising, left the compartment. As he walked along the aisle, his shoulders bumping against the car wall, he scowled at the closed panel of the Darnells' door. If Smokey Darnell was getting fresh with Penny ... When he reached his own car Dan slumped into a seat and stayed there, thinking.

As an outgrowth of that session with himself, Dan sought Penny at the first opportunity, which happened to be after breakfast the next morning. The show had arrived at its new stand, and the cookhouse was raised during the night. Now the big top and all the other tents were going up, and the lot was filled with orderly confusion.

'I want to talk to you,' Dan said briefly, detaching Penny from her companions. 'You got a minute?'

Penny followed Dan away from the cookhouse. 'What is it, Dan?' she asked.

'It's about some talk I've heard,' Dan

answered, choosing exactly the wrong words. 'About you an' Smokey Darnell.'

Penny was no fool and she knew that there was talk about her connection with the Darnell act. There was a sort of caste system with Ruffin's Wild West, as with most shows. The ticket men, advertising men, the 'front-door people' stayed together; the performers were apt to associate with other performers; the laborers, all the population of the long side of the cookhouse, formed a class apart. Even within the castes there was segregation, those members of an act forming a little clique apart from all the others. At first Penny had accompanied Belle and Smokey when they went to a meal or when, between performances, they strolled around the town the show was playing. But recently Smokey had found more and more occasions to be with Penny when his wife was not along. Penny did not like it, but what she did was no business of Dan Mar's. Her voice was cool when she answered.

'And what about me and Smokey Darnell?'

'He's no good,' Dan answered shortly, feeling the antagonism in Penny's voice. 'He's a woman chaser. You've got no business playin' around with him.'

Fools walk where angels fear to tiptoe. The coolness became icy. 'I'm not,' Penny said deliberately, 'playing around with anybody, I'll have you understand, Dan Mar! Smokey

Darnell and Belle have been very kind to me. You're as bad as all the rest around this lot! All you have to do is listen to gossip!'

'Now wait a minute,' Dan expostulated. 'I'm your friend, Penny. I've known you all your life. All I'm tryin' to do is...'

Penny, thoroughly angry, interrupted. 'All you're trying to do is interfere. If it's gossip you're interested in, you ought to listen to some of the things folks say about you and Nevada Warren!'

Dan flushed a slow, dull red, and small danger signals flickered in his eyes. 'An' what are folks sayin' about me an' Nevada?' he drawled.

Penny shrugged. 'I don't repeat gossip,' she answered.

Dan's hand shot out and he seized Penny's shoulder, shaking her roughly. 'Look here!' he rasped. 'You'd better...'

Penny jerked free. 'Keep your hands off me, Dan Mar!' she snapped. 'And let me alone. I'm perfectly able to take care of myself.' She whirled and walked away, skirt swinging angrily. Dan watched her go and he, too, stalked off. Both were angry, and later both were miserable, Penny because she felt dreadfully alone and needed a confidant, someone she could trust; and Dan because, the next time he saw Penny, she was looking up at Smokey Darnell and laughing.

Little by little the act that Dan and Nevada

73

were working out grew into shape. Nevada had an inborn sense of showmanship. She knew when a thing was right and when it was wrong, and Dan learned to defer to her knowledge. They worked during the mornings when the big top was unoccupied. Once or twice Tom Ruffin appeared to watch their progress, and sometimes they had an audience of performers. On a morning some two weeks after the accident which had deprived Nevada of her horse an open break came between Dan and Smokey Darnell.

Nevada and Dan had finished their practice, and Dan returned to the tent for a forgotten rope. As he came through the entry he heard voices and, before he reached the tent, identified them. Smokey was talking to Bob White and Shorty Thoms.

'It's Nevada's act. She makes it. What does Mar do? Spin his rope a little an' that's all. There's nothin' in it for him; it's all built around Nevada.'

'I dunno,' White drawled. 'Dan looks pretty good out there.'

'What does he do that I don't do an' twice as good?' Smokey demanded. 'Nevada's good, I'll give you that, but Mar just ain't there.'

'Mebbe you'd like to team up with Nevada yorese'f, Smokey,' Thoms suggested.

Darnell laughed. 'Me? You've got me wrong, Shorty. The only thing I wonder is what Nevada's gettin' out of this.' He paused a

74

moment, and then his voice went on, filled with innuendo, 'Maybe I don't wonder; maybe I know!' Smokey's laugh was an evil thing.

Dan came out of the entry and without a word climbed the barrier, his errand forgotten. The three men on the benches watched his coming, and Shorty Thoms said: 'Hey, Dan! What ...?'

That was as far as Shorty got. Dan, lean length erect, snarled: 'I heard what you said, Darnell!' and sprang at Smokey's throat.

Smokey Darnell was no pacifist. He came up to meet Dan's charge over the benches and struck two swift, hard blows. Both went home on Dan's face, but Darnell might more profitably have hit the benches themselves. Dan's hands grappled with Smokey's neck and Dan's words rasped harshly in Smokey's ear as they went crashing down together. 'I'll choke the dirty tongue out of you!'

Before the startled Shorty and Bob White could intervene, Dan was in a fair way to make good his threat. Smokey, a little bigger than Dan and perhaps stronger, was futile against the fury that attacked him. Smokey fought with hands and feet and flailing arms, but without result. The hands around his throat were tight hands of steel. Smokey gasped for breath and his heart pounded and he knew a deathly fear. Others, alarmed by the clatter and crash of seats, came running into the tent. Shorty and Bob White tore at Dan, trying to pull him away, and Smokey's face became crimson and his eyes bulged. Finally succeeding, they held Dan, white-faced with fury, still trying to get to Smokey Darnell; and Smokey, reeling back, was caught and supported by Red Halsey and Captain Purrington.

'The dirty lyin' skunk!' Dan panted. 'I'll kill him!'

Purrington took charge, as unruffled and calm as always. 'Get Smokey out of here,' he ordered.

Red Halsey supported the reeling Smokey along the track toward the entrance.

'Dan!' Purrington rasped.

'Damn him!' Dan was still fighting against Shorty and White's restraining arms.

'Dan!'

Gradually sanity returned to Dan's eyes and he quit fighting his captors. Warily Shorty and Bob released their holds.

'What was this about?' Purrington demanded levelly.

'Damn' if I know,' Shorty answered. 'Smokey an' Bob an' me was sittin' here talkin' an' Dan come in. He come right over the barrier an' jumped Smokey.'

Purrington's lips were thin and firm under his narrow gray mustache. 'You come along with me, Dan,' he ordered.

People had a habit of obeying Captain Purrington. He seldom raised his voice, never

76

angrily, but there was something about the grim, gray man, some inborn habit of command, that carried his orders through. Reluctantly Dan moved, and Purrington, walking with him, threw another command over his shoulder. 'Some of you better get those seats up.'

They went to the train and Purrington gestured Dan inside his compartment. Not until the captain had closed the door and nodded toward a chair did he speak.

'You'd better tell me what that was about, Dan. You had a reason for jumping Smokey.'

'He was talkin',' Dan rasped. 'I heard him. I aimed to keep his dirty mouth shut about Nevada.'

Cap Purrington sat down. 'So?' he drawled.

Dan nodded grimly. The anger had drained from him, but in his mind was a cold flame that burned like a sheet across his reason. 'I heard what he said. I stopped him. He'll think twice before he says it again.'

'No.' Purrington shook his head. 'He'll only make sure that you're not around when he says it again. You've made an enemy, Dan.'

Dan shrugged. 'He didn't like me anyhow.'

'Smokey'—Purrington's voice was level—'is a very dangerous man. You'll do well to avoid him.'

'Smokey'—Dan's eyes narrowed—'had better look out for me.'

'Yes,' Purrington nodded thoughtfully, 'he

had. I suppose that Smokey had better look out for you as long as you face him. But you must watch your back.'

'I'll watch it,' Dan assured.

Purrington smiled. 'You don't know how,' he drawled. 'What else was it, Dan? There's something else between you and Smokey.'

'I suppose there is,' Dan answered reflectively. 'I don't like him. I never have. An' I don't like the way he's always with Penny.'

'Tell me,' the captain ordered softly.

Dan found himself talking. Not just about Penny and Smokey Darnell, but about Penny and himself and Carl. The captain listened, produced a thin cigar and, lighting it, leaned back on the bed. For the first time Dan had an audience, someone he could talk to, someone who listened and did not ask questions, with whom he did not have to be on guard. Gradually he eased, the tension leaving his mind as well as his muscles.

'I see,' Purrington said. 'You feel responsible for Penny. You think that if you hadn't left them, Carl would be alive. You're mistaken, Dan. Those things happen. It was Carl's time to die.'

'Do you believe that, Cap?'

'I believe that when a man's time is up, it's up,' Purrington said with conviction.

For a time there was quiet and Dan looked around the little room. Few people ever visited Captain Purrington in his car. The

78

compartment was comfortable, the bed made, the floor clean. There was a stand of guns against a wall, and under the bed the end of a case showed. Purrington kept his pistols in the case; Dan had seen it often. Above the stand of guns was a long, unglassed frame backed by plush to which were pinned numerous medals. In the lower right-hand corner of the case Dan saw a familiar object, a small gold saddle with silver stirrups.

'Where did you get this, Captain?' he asked, rising and touching the saddle.

'Ruffin gave it to me,' Purrington answered absently.

'Carl had one like it,' Dan said.

Purrington nodded. 'Ruffin had four of them,' he said. 'He got us all in his office and passed them out.'

'Got who in the car?'

'Carl and Darnell and me. He kept one himself. We'd had a good year, and Tom picked the saddles up in Mexico when we played El Paso; had them made to order.'

'Then,' Dan drawled, 'there aren't a lot of other saddles like that?'

'Just four that I know of. What makes you so interested, Dan?'

'Penny gave Carl's to me.'

Purrington nodded. 'I see.'

Dan walked back to the chair and sat down. Purrington stared at him thoughtfully and then shook his head. 'I'm going to give you a piece

79

of advice,' he said. 'Usually I don't give advice. It's the cheapest thing there is, and the least useful. I hope you'll follow what I tell you, but I'm afraid you won't. Don't mix into things that are other people's business. That's a part you won't follow. Don't ever become too fond of anyone. That's the way to get hurt. You'll not heed that either, but I hope you will heed this: Don't ever turn your back to Smokey Darnell.'

Rising, Dan said, 'Thanks a lot, Captain. I'll try to remember that. Especially that last.' He grinned and tenderly touched an eye. 'Smokey got in one good lick, anyhow. So long, Captain.'

'Good-by, Dan. Don't forget what I've told you.'

'I won't,' Dan promised.

CHAPTER SIX

Everyone on the lot heard of the clash between Dan Mar and Smokey Darnell. At dinner Dan sported a black eye that discolored all his cheek, but Darnell did not come to the cookhouse at all. Penny, viewing the black eye, walked by Dan with stiffly lifted chin, and at the table Dan heard her comment: 'Fighting! Just like any roustabout!' It did not help his digestion.

After the meal Nevada intercepted her partner and surveyed him critically. 'That's a honey of a mouse,' she commented.

Dan had a horn drooped. 'Yeah,' he answered. 'I got it fightin', just like any common roustabout.'

'Must have been a nice fight,' Nevada drawled. 'I see that Smokey didn't come to dinner. You come along with me and I'll fix that eye.'

'It don't need fixin'.'

'You don't want to go on looking like that,' Nevada said.

'Maybe I won't go on at all.'

'Oh yes, you will. Come on; I'll fix that eye.'

Reluctantly Dan followed Nevada to the dressing rooms and waited while she brought her make-up kit and repaired the damaged eye and cheek with grease paint.

'There!' Nevada said when she was finished. 'What was the scrap about, Dan?'

'Smokey gave up too much head, an' I heard him.'

Nevada's eyes twinkled. 'Was it about Penny?'

'No.'

'Then,' Nevada stated firmly, 'it was about me.'

Dan did not answer, and Nevada chuckled. 'I told you a long time ago that they couldn't say anything about me that hadn't been said,' she reminded. 'You needn't fight on my account.'

'Nobody,' Dan stated curtly, 'is goin' to talk about you an' get away with it. Not when I'm around. You're swell, Nevada.'

'Do you think so?' Nevada eyed her partner.

'You know I do.'

Nevada laughed again. 'You're pretty swell yourself, Danny,' she said, for the first time using a diminutive of Dan's name. 'Better get into costume now.'

'O.K.,' Dan agreed. 'Say, Nevada, would you go uptown with me after the show tonight? Maybe we could get a snack some place.'

'I'll go with you,' Nevada replied. 'Now go on, Dan. You don't want to be late for the entry.'

Dan strode off, and Nevada stood at the door of the dressing rooms, her make-up box in her hands. Penny arrived at the tent to dress, and Nevada grinned at her.

'I've been repairing Dan,' she announced. 'How is Smokey getting along? Does he need some fixing?'

Penny bristled. She had just come from the Darnells' compartment. 'He's not going on,' she answered stiffly. 'Dan Mar is a fool. He had no reason to attack Smokey!'

'No?' Nevada's eyes narrowed. 'He should have jumped Smokey a long time ago. You're playing with fire, Penny.'

'How do you mean?'

'I mean that Dan thinks a lot of you and that

Smokey Darnell is a bad customer.'

Penny flushed in anger. 'Smokey and Belle have been good to me,' she retorted. 'Dan certainly showed how much he thought of me. Smokey's my best friend, and all Dan has done is to get me talked about.'

'You could have worked an act with Dan when you joined the show,' Nevada reminded. 'Why didn't you?'

'It happens to be none of your business'— Penny's answer was elaborate—'but I'll tell you. I didn't want to work with Dan, and Smokey wrote to me offering me a place in his act.'

'And so,' Nevada drawled, 'that gives you a right to treat Dan like dirt. You hardly talk to him. That boy likes you, Penny.'

'I have a right to choose my own friends!' Penny's head was high. 'If you think so much of Dan Mar, why don't you go with him? You're together all the time anyhow.'

Nevada's eyes narrowed. 'Maybe I will,' she drawled thoughtfully, and started into the tent. Just at the door she turned. 'If you're interested,' she completed, 'I'll tell you that Dan didn't jump Smokey because of you. Smokey was using his dirty mouth on me when Dan shut him up. You can tell your friends that, if you're afraid of scandal.'

Nevada disappeared, and Penny stared angrily after her. Nevada Warren was thirty years old if she was a day, perhaps thirty-five.

She was getting hippy, and she certainly stuck her nose into other people's affairs. So Dan had been fighting over Nevada, had he? Well, she was welcome to him! Penny sailed into the dressing tent.

After the show that night Nevada and Dan sat in a little restaurant and talked. In the way that only a woman can, Nevada pried information from Dan and learned just what had been said. She frowned when Dan reported Smokey's estimate of Dan's portion of the act but did not comment. Before they left the restaurant Dan was grinning, and Nevada, sparkling beside him, said: 'I like you when you smile, Dan. You don't do it often enough.'

'Mebbe,' Dan answered, 'I'd do it oftener if you were around.'

There was an extra on the street, and while the two waited for a streetcar to take them back to the show grounds they heard a newsboy crying it: 'Collector murdered! Read all about it! Street-railway collector murdered. Paper! Paper, mister?'

Dan shook his head. He did not care to read about a murder.

The next morning, working in the arena with Domino and Nigger, Nevada halted the rehearsal. 'I don't like this,' she announced. 'See here, Dan. Suppose you try this stunt?' Nevada described what she had in mind, and as she talked Dan's eyes brightened.

'I don't know if I can do it or not,' he said,

'but I'll try. And look, Nevada. Suppose we finish this way: If I can roll a loop that big I can spin a wedding ring. We could finish with that.'

'Try it!' Nevada ordered.

Dan walked back toward the center of the arena, straightening his rope, and Nevada took Nigger and Domino to the far end. Red Halsey, entering the arena, came limping up to Dan. The Rocker horse still did not know that bucking was just an act and had thrown Red hard during the evening performance.

'Look, Dan.' Red halted beside him. 'Do me a favor, will you?'

'Sure.' Dan coiled the rope.

'I'm layin' off today. I think that damned Rocker broke my neck. Will you take my place in the stage holdup?'

Dan flipped out a loop. 'Yeah,' he agreed. 'Watch this, Red. We're goin' to try somethin'.'

'You'll have to get a mask an' a gun from Brannigan,' Red informed, stepping back. 'He'll pass 'em out before the spec.'

'I'll get 'em.' Dan's eyes were on Nevada. 'Step back a little, Red.'

Red moved further away, and Dan began to build a loop, spinning it above his head, making it grow.

'Go!' he called.

Nevada, riding Nigger and leading Domino beside her, came charging down the arena, and Dan brought the big loop down and rolled it

85

out. The horses and rider went through, but Domino's hind foot caught on the loop and it collapsed.

'Try it again, Dan,' Nevada called, riding back. 'That wasn't your fault. See if you can make your loop a little bigger.'

'I'll try,' Dan answered.

That afternoon, equipping himself to take Red's place in the stage-holdup spectacle. Dan sought Brannigan, the property man. In Ruffin's Wild West, properties were checked in and out at every performance. Ruffin took no chances on a gun's being loaded with other than blank cartridges, and he eliminated property loss by the checking system.

Brannigan gave Dan a belt and filled holster and looked for a mask but failed to find one. 'Dawggone,' he drawled. 'Now where'd I put that? Dawggone!'

Further search failed to disclose the mask. The other stage holdups had already checked out their properties and were waiting.

'You'll just have to use a bandanna,' Brannigan announced. 'There ain't time to git a mask made.'

'All right,' Dan agreed.

He rode to the entry where already the stagecoach was standing. In the entryway the bandits adjusted their masks, and as Dan tied Bob White's mask in place he paused to examine it. The mask had been made for service. Of black silk, the mask's eyeholes had been reinforced and the tie strings bound on the edges.

'Come on, tie it on,' White ordered. 'Ruffin's makin' the spiel.'

The stage was duly held up, the sheriff's posse arriving amidst much shooting to drive off the bandits.

'Who makes the masks?' Dan asked when he returned belt and pistol to the property man.

'Mrs. Flarity.'

Dan found Mrs. Flarity in her room in the prop tent. The wardrobe mistress had a sewing machine going, and she finished her stitching before she looked up. An institution of Ruffin's show, Mary Flarity 'took no lip from nobody.'

'Yes?' she greeted.

'About that mask ...' Dan began.

'Oh, so you're the one who lost it?' Mrs. Flarity shrilled. 'Always makin' work for me. I had to make new ones when the season started, an' now another. Careless! That's what you are!'

'But I didn't lose it,' Dan defended, grinning. 'I just wanted to see how you made them. Do you always make 'em that way?'

'An' why not? It's as good a way as any.'

'Sure it is, Mary,' Dan answered, and left the tent hastily. Mary Flarity was 'Mrs. Flarity' to the show people, and she resented the use of her first name.

From the property tent Dan went to the

87

train. The mail was in, and Red Halsey had a letter for Dan. Following his mother's round, almost girlish writing, Dan gathered the news of Brule and Tejon and of the MY. There was almost as much news in what Clara did not say as in what she said. The cattle were doing well. Slim Colson was still working at the place. Bruce was hiring hay crews and had bought a new mower. The Daisy mare had lost her colt. All the little happenings, the small, homely touches, were of interest to Dan, but there was one item missing. Save for the mention of the hay crew, Clara Mar did not speak of her husband.

Dan refolded the letter and placed it in the envelope. Bruce was still angry, adhering strictly to his law and letter. He wanted no word of his son and he wanted his son to have no word of him.

A letter from home always made Dan feel low. His mother wrote regularly, and Dan answered the letters promptly, generally including the show's itinerary and always putting his own return address on the envelope. Now he brought out his stationery and, with a tablet on his knee, moistened his pencil and began.

It was easy enough to write his mother. Dan included all the things of interest that he knew: told about the towns they played, mentioned the progress in his act, gave Clara news of those persons whom she knew. When he had finished that letter and had addressed and sealed the envelope he began another. Dan had promised to inform Art Murrah of anything he might learn or remember concerning the Brule bank robbery. Certainly the fact that the masks worn in Ruffin's Wild West were identical with those discarded by the bank robbers came under that heading. He wrote thoughtfully, stopping now and then to chew on his pencil.

When the second letter was finished Dan borrowed stamps from Red, then spoke to the car in general. 'Anybody got mail to go? I'm goin' uptown.'

Several of the men gave letters to Dan and he left the car. As he reached the ground he heard Ruffin call to him, and Dan made his way back to the end of the train.

'I want to talk to you,' Ruffin said, 'Come on in.'

Entering the car, Dan waited impatiently while the show owner seated himself. 'Put yore letters in the basket,' Ruffin directed. 'There'll be mail goin' in to town pretty soon.' And then: 'Dan, you had a fight with Smokey Darnell yesterday.'

Dan placed his envelopes in the basket on Ruffin's desk. 'That's right,' he answered.

'It won't do!' Ruffin shook his big head. 'I can't have that around the show.'

'Then,' Dan drawled levelly, 'tell Darnell to keep his mouth shut about me an' Nevada.'

'You an' Nevada?' Ruffin appeared startled.

'Me an' Nevada.'

Ruffin stared at Dan. 'I heard it different,' the big man said. 'I heard that Smokey made some cracks about yore ropin'.'

'He did. He made some other cracks too. I stopped him.'

Ruffin's fingers tapped the desk top. Suddenly he looked up. 'You lay off of Smokey,' he ordered. 'I'll tell him to lay off you. An' if he makes a break about Nevada ...' Ruffin left the threat unfinished.

'He won't,' Dan said positively. 'Not any more.'

Ruffin grinned. 'They tell me you kind of choked him. All right, that's all, Dan. Remember, lay off Smokey.'

'As long as he steers clear of me,' Dan promised, and went out.

When Dan had gone Ruffin walked to the car ahead where the front-door people had their quarters. Here were the ticket sellers, the doormen, Fred Kerr the bookkeeper, all those who looked after the business end of the show. Ruffin spoke to Kerr.

'I'm goin' to the white wagon, Fred. If anybody wants me I'll be there.'

*　　　*　　　*

Dan, leaving the train, walked to the lot. The long summer twilight had descended, and the lot was quiet save for the distant clatter in the cookhouse.

Nodding to two men in the pad room, Dan walked on back to the chest that still bore Carl Thwaite's name stenciled upon it. Sitting down upon it, Dan picked up a spur that he had dropped after the performance. Idly he turned the spur in his hands and then spun the rowel with his forefinger. The rowel buzzed around like the thoughts in Dan's mind.

Had he, Dan wondered, done the right thing in writing to Murrah? Had he made trouble for Tom Ruffin? He hoped not. Ruffin had been good to him, had given him a chance to get away from the narrow, trying confines of the MY. Just because a few pieces of silk resembled each other was no reason to suppose that they came from the same place. Ruffin might have discarded the masks the robbers wore; they might have been stolen; they might have resembled each other by coincidence. Dan scowled. Anyhow, it was too late to do anything about it; the letter was gone. Dan spun the spur rowel again.

He wished, sometimes, that he had never joined the show. Movement, irregular hours, the excitement, had all been fine at first, but they were getting a little old. The broad reaches of the MY pastures appeared in Dan's imagination; the click of mowers in the hay meadows and the hot, sweet smell of the new-cut grass came back to him. He wondered how the cattle were doing. He wondered about

Bruce. He wished that Clara had told him about Bruce. Dan scowled. Bruce didn't give a damn about his son. Why should he, Dan Mar, worry? The spur rowel buzzed again.

Maybe if Carl were alive it would be different. If he were working an act with Carl and Penny it would be all right. He wouldn't be so lonesome and weary of the show. Maybe it would be different when he and Nevada got this act going. Nevada was surely a good scout, frank and square and always on the level. She was like Penny; like Carl too. Reaching into his shirt, Dan withdrew the little saddle that Penny had given him. He wore it on a cord around his neck, against his chest. Turning the small carved piece of gold, he could read Carl's name engraved on the back. The cord was blackened and frayed a little where the gold rubbed. He would, Dan thought as he returned the tiny saddle to its hiding place, get a leather string to replace the worn cord.

As the people of the show streamed toward the cookhouse Dan rose and, buckling the spur leathers, hung them to the horn of the saddle that had once belonged to Carl Thwaite. Stretched along the length of the pad room was a rack filled with saddles, the property of men and women who lived and played and worked. It was queer, Dan thought as he looked at the saddles, how inanimate things stayed on after the man who owned them was dead. Carl's saddle and Carl's spurs, for instance: Would someone else have them when Dan, too, was gone? No doubt but that Carl had looked forward to owning many pairs of spurs, more than this one saddle. Idly Dan's fingers traced the spur tracks across the saddle's seat, and then, lifting the spurs from the horn, he fitted a rowel against the tracks and followed them lightly. The rowel did not fit the tracks. The points were too close together and there was a gap in the tracks where a broken prong had missed marking the leather. The spur in Dan's hand had no broken rowel prong. Dan tried the other spur. Like its fellow, it had no broken prong and the rowel points were too close to fit the tracks.

Replacing the spurs on the saddle horn, Dan opened the chest and produced the other pair of spurs. A glance showed him that these would not fit the tracks either. The rowels were big, with square, blunt points that would cut leather, not stamp it with a series of perforations. Thoughtfully Dan dropped the spurs back into the chest and closed the lid.

Carl had owned only two pairs of spurs. Dan was sure that he had bought all of Carl's tack. For a full, long minute he stood staring at the saddle. Carl Thwaite had not worn the spurs that made those tracks across the saddle seat, those tracks made on the day Carl died. Spurs and tracks did not match, and so by no chance could Carl have made them. And if Carl had not made the tracks, a question remained:

93

Who *had* made them ... and why?

CHAPTER SEVEN

It so happened that on the morning of the fight between Dan Mar and Smokey Darnell, Penny was not on the lot. She had gone to town, shopping, and, returning just at noon, the first person she met was Ruth Shattuck, who reported the altercation. Fighting was not uncommon on the Ruffin's Wild West lot. Hostlers, canvasmen, and roustabouts are not peaceful people, and many a difference of opinion was settled with fists; but the performers, as a rule, did not do battle. Hence, when Penny saw Dan Mar's black eye she made her unfortunate remark.

When lunch was over Penny and Ruth left the cookhouse to walk to the train, and Ruth, perhaps a trifle jealous, perhaps only because of the ingrained feline which lies dormant in any woman, retailed a little gossip. There were many interpolations of: 'I'm your friend, Penny, or I wouldn't tell you this,' and 'I'm being perfectly frank with you, Penny.' By the time they reached the train Penny hated Ruth heartily.

The girls parted at the cars, and Penny, because she was Penny and loyal, went to the Darnell compartment. Belle Darnell met her at the door.

'Is Smokey hurt badly?' Penny asked. 'I was uptown and just came back. That's why I haven't been here.'

Belle, a thin, dark woman with smoldering eyes, shook her head. 'He's not hurt,' she said briefly.

'Can I see him?'

'No!' The smoldering eyes studied Penny's face. Belle laughed suddenly. 'He got about what he had coming,' she said. 'You're just a fool little kid, aren't you?'

Penny was amazed by the question. Belle's voice was hoarse. 'And all the time I've been thinking ...' she began, and then: 'All that's wrong with Smokey is that his neck's sore. We won't put on the act this afternoon.'

'Belle!' Smokey's voice came petulantly through the closed compartment door. 'Come here.'

Belle nodded to Penny and, answering the summons, closed the door behind her. Penny stared at it and then, leaving the car, went back toward the lot, walking slowly. At the dressing tent she met Nevada Warren, holding her make-up kit and watching Dan Mar walk toward the pad room.

Penny's interview with Nevada was brief. Thoroughly angry, she followed Nevada into the tent and all during the performance she stored up anger against Dan. After the show, had she found Dan, the anger would have boiled over, but he was not in evidence when Penny searched the lot, and she would not go to the bachelor car to find him. Before the evening performance Penny visited the Darnells again, but Smokey was gone.

'He went uptown to see a doctor about his neck,' Belle reported.

Penny wondered fleetingly why Smokey had not consulted the physician whom Tom Ruffin carried with the show. That wonder passed, for Belle, looking at her searchingly, drawled: 'You like Smokey, don't you?'

'I like you both,' Penny answered. 'You've been awfully good to me, Belle.'

'Yeah?' Belle's black eyes searched Penny's face. 'I wonder if I have been good to you.'

'What do you mean, Belle?'

Belle laughed harshly. 'I don't know what I mean,' she answered. 'Why don't you get out and put on an act of your own, Penny? Why do you stick around with Smokey and me?'

'Don't you want me, Belle?' Penny asked.

'No, I don't,' Belle said bluntly. 'I was sorry for you, kid, and when Smokey said we'd take you in the act I thought it was all right. He's a smooth devil, damn him!'

'Why, Belle!'

'Surprised you, didn't I, kid?' Belle met Penny's eyes. 'I meant that. I wish I wasn't in love with Smokey. I'd like to hate him!'

'Belle!' Penny got up and took a step toward the other woman.

'You go on,' Belle rasped. 'Get out of here, Penny. Leave me alone!'

Bewildered and totally unable to find a reason for this outburst, Penny left the compartment. That evening she put on her costume and was ready for the act, but Belle and Smokey did not appear. Penny rode in the grand entry, acted as a stagecoach passenger, and appeared in the finale. She saw that Dan was at work as usual and resolved to see him, but after the show Dan and Nevada went off together, another small, sharp thorn among the many that pricked Penny's mind.

The next morning after breakfast, for which Smokey appeared, urbane as usual, Penny left the cookhouse and started toward the train, and Smokey, catching up with her, tucked his hand familiarly beneath her arm. 'I want to talk to you, Penny,' he said. 'Let's go where we won't be bothered.'

Unwillingly Penny allowed Darnell to lead her toward the stock tent. They stopped behind the stock top where hay and grain sacks had been piled. The morning feeding was finished, and the hostlers were inside the tent, grooming.

'Look, Penny,' Smokey said persuasively. 'Belle blew up last night. She told me what she said. You mustn't mind her. She isn't feeling good.'

'Is she sick?' Penny's eyes showed her concern.

'No,' Darnell answered. 'She just doesn't

feel good. She's nervous. I think I'll have to let Belle rest awhile. Do you think you and I could swing the act together?'

'Why ... I suppose so. But Belle...'

'Never mind about Belle for a minute.' Smokey put his hand on Penny's arm. 'Let's talk about you and me. You like me, don't you, Penny?'

'Yes,' Penny answered frankly. 'You've been good to me, Smokey. You're the best friend I've had since Carl died.'

Darnell nodded. 'I've tried to be,' he said. 'Now, Penny, don't you think that you ought to be a little nicer to me than you have been?'

'What do you mean?' Penny was frightened by what she saw in Darnell's eyes.

'I mean a little more friendly. I'm going to send Belle back to Ruffin's place. Don't you think that you and I could hit it off together?' Smokey squeezed Penny's arm.

Penny pulled the arm away. 'I've got to go,' she said. 'I can't stay here, Smokey. I ... Please let me go!'

Darnell had caught her arm again. 'You're a sweet kid,' he said thickly, drawing Penny toward him. 'Don't be scared, Penny.'

'Let me go!' Penny snapped. 'If I told Dan Mar...'

Darnell's eyes narrowed as he released the girl. 'Tell Mar!' he rasped. 'I'm fixed for him. All I want is for him to start something with me.' He lifted his hand and touched his left armpit. Penny's fascinated eyes saw the outline of a holster beneath Smokey's shirt. 'Look here, have you been fooling with me? Have you been giving me the come-on?'

'What do you mean?'

'You know what I mean! You've hung around me plenty. You haven't been backward about letting me take you out to eat or going places with me. Why do you think I took you in the act? Because I needed you? Why, you little fool! ... That's what you did think!' Again rough hands caught Penny's arms, pulling her close.

Penny struggled and then, unable to win free, kicked viciously. Her boot toe went home on Smokey Darnell's shin.

'Damn you!' he rasped, releasing the girl. 'I'll...'

Penny did not hear the threat. She ran, as fast as she could, toward the end of the stock tent. Reaching it, she slowed and looked back over her shoulder. She could not run across the lot and seek refuge in the car as she wanted to do; she could not attract attention to herself. Seeing Smokey come limping from behind the tent, she increased her pace and sought the safety of the room she shared with Ruth Shattuck.

Fortunately Ruth was not in. Penny threw herself down on the bed and wept, long, racking sobs that tore at her, voicing her fear and her loathing. She felt unclean, as though she had been soiled. Ruth, entering the compartment, paused a moment and then dropped down to the bed and put her arm over Penny's shoulders.

'What's the matter?' Ruth demanded. 'What is it, Penny?'

Sobs were the only answer. Ruth patted the slim, heaving shoulders. 'Now, Penny,' she comforted, 'it isn't that bad, honey. Please, Penny. What's the matter, dear?'

Gradually the sobbing quieted, but Penny's tear-stained face remained buried in the pillow. Ruth stood up.

'I'm going to tell Smokey that you can't work today,' she announced. 'You stay quiet, honey. I'll bring you a tray from the cookhouse. You just stay here and rest.'

Penny remained on the bed. Ruth came back and tried to talk with her, but Penny would not talk. She refused to let Ruth bring her food from the cookhouse and that afternoon stayed in the car, hearing the strains of band music from the big top and through the window seeing the movement on the show grounds. After the show Ruth returned with practical suggestions concerning a hot bath and tea and with the threat that she would get the show's doctor. Penny dissuaded her.

'I don't need the doctor, Ruth. I'll be all right. Please just leave me alone.'

Ruth adjusted the shades, covered Penny, and went out again. A woman herself, she knew the vagaries of other women. Long after Ruth was gone Penny lay thinking. Finally she rose and went to the dressing room at the end of the car.

Cold water and make-up helped. Penny dressed her hair and then, leaving the room, went in search of Tom Ruffin.

Ruffin was not in his car. Fred Kerr, collecting mail from the letter basket, said that the boss had gone to the white wagon. Penny started across the lot toward the entrance of the big top, and a voice hailed her.

'Wait a minute, Penny. I'll walk with you.'

Penny hesitated, and Captain Purrington's long legs brought him abreast. 'Missed you this afternoon,' Purrington announced cheerfully. 'Ruth said that you were under the weather. I ... What's the matter, Penny? You've been crying!'

Penny lifted red-rimmed, tear-filled eyes to the captain's face. She saw sympathy there, and more. Behind the gray eyes were understanding and strength. 'Oh, Captain,' Penny wailed, 'I don't know what to do. I've got to get away. I've got to leave the show. What can I do?'

Purrington's hand was firm on Penny's elbow as he turned her. 'You,' Captain Purrington announced, 'are coming back to the car with me and tell me all about it.'

In Purrington's compartment Penny was seated on the bed. The small glass of wine the captain brought warmed the girl and steadied her nerves. At first she was reluctant and would not answer the gentle questions that the man asked, but presently the reluctance broke and Penny told her story, ending it with a question.

'I can't stay with the show. What will I do, Captain?'

The lean gray man stared out of the window where now dusk was falling. 'You've got a living to make,' he said slowly. 'You don't know anything but show work. I wish ...' The captain did not say what he wished.

'If only I'd gone into an act with Dan when I first came back,' Penny said wistfully, 'none of this would have happened. But it's too late now. Dan and Nevada are working together. I'm afraid. If you had seen his eyes when he said he wanted me to tell Dan ... He's got a gun. It's under his shirt. He wants Dan to say something to him. He'll kill Dan. He'll ...' Penny's voice rose on a hysterical note.

'Take it easy!' Purrington rapped the command. 'You won't say anything to Dan about this. You'd just make trouble. I've got an idea, Penny. I need to dress up my act a little. How would you like to work with me? You could set the targets and throw the glass balls and do all that, couldn't you? Sure you could. I'd rather have you than the boy I've got working now. I'll fix it up for you.'

'Could I?' Penny stared at the captain's calm, grave face.

102

'Of course you could. I'll fix it up with Ruffin. Why, you've already done most of the act with me, up at the ranch.'

'But ... what will I do about Smokey and Belle?'

'I'll talk to Smokey,' Purrington said evenly, a trace of iron under the level tone. 'I think Smokey will understand how things are when I get through. He'll leave you alone. Now, Penny, you wash your face and powder your nose, and you and I will go uptown to eat supper.'

'But'—Penny got up from the bed—'what will I tell Dan? He'll ask me why I've changed. And what about Smokey? He means to kill Dan, Captain.'

'Tell Dan that I've hired you in my act,' Purrington answered. 'And don't worry about Smokey at all. Just forget about him. He won't harm Dan, I'll give you my word. Now run on and get ready. I'll meet you right by your car.'

Penny, with all the weight of the world lifted from her young shoulders, stopped beside the door. Purrington smiled at her and, because of her relief and the kindness of this gray, grim man, Penny took two quick steps, threw her arms around the captain's neck, and kissed him.

'You don't know ...' she exclaimed. 'I can't thank you, Captain!'

'Run on now!' Purrington ordered sternly. 'Don't keep me waiting!'

103

'Oh, I won't. I won't, Captain! I'll be ready!' Penny fled.

When she was gone Captain Purrington gently touched his cheek where Penny's lips had brushed, then, rising, shook his clothes in place and picked up his hat. He did not believe in postponing events, and now was as good a time as any to interview Smokey Darnell.

*　　*　　*

After the performance that night Dan cornered Ruth Shattuck. He had missed Penny at both the afternoon and evening shows. Penny, Ruth said, was all right, just a little upset. 'You don't need to worry, Dan.' Ruth's smile was both bright and malicious. 'There's nothing wrong. And anyhow, Penny's not your partner. Smokey's the one to worry.'

The night was hot. Gradually the cars quieted. Dan, restless and unable to sleep, listened to Red Halsey's steady snoring across the aisle and finally, unable to bear it longer, got up and dressed. Carrying his boots to the car platform, he donned them and walked toward the lot. Lights gleamed from Ruffin's and Purrington's windows. Evidently others were as restless as Dan Mar.

The lot was dark. The big top loomed against the lighter sky, a great pyramid of canvas, and behind it squatted the other tents, smaller blotches in the night. Dan had never seen the show like this, sleeping, resting from the day. A light flashed against canvas, traveling along a wall. Dan was instantly alert and then grinned to himself. One of the watchmen, making his rounds, had flashed a bull's-eye lantern on a tent side, that was all. No cause for alarm. For a while longer he watched the tents, waiting for a repetition of the flash. When it did not come he turned and went slowly back to the train.

It had not been a watchman's bull's-eye flashing light against a tent side that Dan had seen. In the pad room three men sat on a chest, their voices low in the gloom.

'They've got that mask,' a man rasped. 'The damn collector had it in his hand. Why did you get so close to him, Bugs? If you'd stayed where you belonged he'd never got it off your face.'

'How did I know the damned fool would take a chance?' The answering voice was surly. 'Anyhow, even if he did see me he won't tell about it.'

'Killin'!' the first man snarled. 'I don't like killin'. Robbery's bad enough, but when they've got murder on you...'

A third voice, smooth, drawling, interposed a word. 'There's no use cryin' about it now. He got the mask an' he's dead. You haven't seen anything funny around the show, have you? No cops, nothin' like that?'

'No, I ain't.'

'That's good.'

There was a little silence, and then the third man spoke again. 'I told you boys I wanted to see you. Somethin's come up.'

'What?'

'You know Dan Mar?'

'Of course we know Dan Mar!' The man called Bugs snapped the statement. 'What about him?'

'He was in the bank at Brule, remember?'

'Sure I remember. We threw him in the vault with the rest, didn't we?'

'That's right. Well, Mar wrote a letter to Murrah, the sheriff back at Brule. I took the mail uptown this evenin'. I saw Mar's name on the envelope and I wondered what he was writin' Murrah about, so I opened the letter.'

'Well?'

'Well, Mr. Mar was writin' Murrah about some masks he'd found. He told Murrah that the masks we wore when we took the Stockman's Bank had come from Ruffin's show.'

Dead silence. Then Bugs said: 'The hell!'

'I didn't,' the third speaker said, 'mail the letter. Naturally!' He laughed.

'Mar was in here this afternoon,' the second man growled. 'Sittin' on his chest. I was talkin' to the pad-room boss.'

'It don't make no difference where he *was*,' Bugs drawled. 'It's where he's goin' that interests me. What do you boys think?'

'I think he's gettin' too damned nosy!'

'An' so do I.' The third speaker's voice was still easy and level. 'We're goin' to get rid of Mr. Mar before he gets his nose clear into our business. But we've got to be careful. We can't have a lot of cops come down on the show. We've got too good a thing to blow it up.'

'So?' Bugs prompted.

'So now,' the third man answered, 'we'll make a plan for Dan Mar.'

CHAPTER EIGHT

A stand at a state fair was an event in the itinerary of Ruffin's Wild West, and the routing was arranged to strike as many fair towns as possible. There are always good crowds at a fair, people who have come to town to display their own products, to see what the rest of the state is doing, to spend money, and to have a good time. Conversely, fair managements like to have a show or carnival as an added attraction.

Ruffin's Wild West, arriving at midmorning, unloaded and hauled to the lot. All morning long wagons shuttled between the railroad yards and the fairgrounds at the edge of town, and after the tops were up there was a parade.

Dan was nervous, for this stand was to see the first public performance of the act. Tom Ruffin, watching the final rehearsal, had grunted approval, and Nevada assured Dan that they were 'in.' Still, until the final verdict of a crowd was given, neither performer could be sure. Nevada was as nervous as her partner, but she masked her feelings.

Ruffin had scheduled the act midway in the show, and at Nevada's insistence they were to work alone with nothing in the arena or on the track to detract attention from them. Waiting for Nevada to arrive, Dan stood in the entry that night and scarcely saw the performance in the tent. The show ran smoothly, and the crowd, come to be entertained, was friendly. Nevada came up behind him, and Dan turned, his eyes widening as he looked at the girl.

During all the time of rehearsal Nevada had worn a practice costume, a black blouse and tight black trousers with straps that ran beneath her shoes. Now she was dressed in glittering white silk tights and bodice. A cape covered her shoulders, and her hair, coal black and short, caught and reflected the light from the big top.

The girl laughed at the amazement she read on Dan's face. 'You didn't think I was going to wear a practice costume, did you?' she demanded.

'No, but ...' Dan looked down at his own costume, typical showman clothes: boots, spurs, dark trousers, a flamboyant blue silk shirt, a neckerchief, and a big gray hat.

'You're all right,' Nevada said coolly,

discarding her cape. 'Get ready.'

Using Dan's cupped hand for a mounting block, Nevada went lightly up to the equestrian's pad that Domino carried in place of a saddle. Dan mounted Nigger, his coiled ropes on his saddle horn, while in the arena Tom Ruffin roared announcement through his megaphone.

'Your attention, please! Ladies and gentlemen, the next act, a feature attraction of this performance, will be Nevada Warren and Dan Mar: The Cowboy and the Lady. Nevada Warren and Dan Mar!' Ruffin swung his hat and the band blared.

Nevada flashed a reassuring smile at Dan. 'Good luck!' she said.

'Good luck,' Dan answered, and the horses moved.

As she cleared the entrance Nevada stood up on the pad, a straight, slim figure in shining silk, and Dan, waiting briefly, followed her, his rope swinging as he built a loop.

They had based the act on two factors: Dan's roping and Nevada's ability as an equestrienne. The girl was a graceful white flame that danced and pirouetted on Domino's back, and Dan was a colorful demon pursuing her, throwing his loops to entrap the flame. Domino kept an even pace around the arena, following a predesigned pattern, and Nigger, always on the inside of the pattern, held a fixed distance. Dan's loops rolled out and Nevada

109

danced through them, jumped them, tumbled through them. It was artistry, beautiful to watch because it seemed so effortless. Dan dismounted, and Nigger trotted to the end of the arena while the man pursued the girl on foot and Domino stopped short, the big, circling loop settling about him. Domino jumped the lifeless rope, and as Dan gathered it in the appaloosa and his rider joined Nigger. Dan built a big loop, let it grow, jumped through it, raised it and widened it. Nevada, one foot now on Domino's pad, the other on Nigger's saddle, came down the arena as the loop rolled out. Horses and girl went through and Nevada circled back. Dan touched the pad, went up like a cat, and stood balancing himself while the horses circled the tent. As he balanced he spun his loop, widening it above his head. The loop settled and circled the horses as, side by side, they made their exit.

In the stands the crowd roared. Ruffin shouted through the megaphone to announce the next act, but the crowd would have none of it. They wanted to Cowboy and the Lady. In the entrance Nevada laughed up at Dan and her lips moved, the words lost in the tumult. Dan bent close.

'Go back, Dan. We'll take our bows. We've stopped the show, Danny. We've stopped the show.'

Leading their horses, Dan and Nevada entered again and bowed. Whoops, whistles, stamping feet, and a thunderburst of clapping greeted them. They retired and were called back again and then again.

Ruffin, at the entrance shouted: 'Spin the weddin' ring again,' and so, mounting, they circled the arena once more, Dan's loop spinning slowly about both horses. Only then would the crowd let the show go on.

In the entrance Nevada slipped down from her horse to join Dan, already on the ground. He did not see Penny Thwaite, standing well back in the entrance beside Red Halsey; he did not see Smokey Darnell looking at him with dark, slitted eyes, nor Belle, nor any of the performers who came crowding around, nor Tom Ruffin pushing through to join him. He saw only Nevada's face, her sparkling eyes, her cheeks, redder because of the flush beneath the rouge, and her lips, parted as she smiled, showing even white teeth. In that instant Nevada Warren was beautiful.

'We did it, Danny!' the girl exulted. 'We stopped the show!' Rising on tiptoe, she threw her arms about Dan's neck and kissed him.

'Here!' Tom Ruffin rasped. 'Just because you stopped the show is no reason you can do that. It went over, Nevada. It went over big. I'll sign a contract.'

Nevada turned from Dan to Ruffin. 'You bet you'll sign a contract,' she laughed. 'For a good stiff salary. It did go over, didn't it, Tom? We were good, weren't we?'

111

'You sure were,' Ruffin answered. 'An' now will you folks kindly get to hell out of the entrance? We've got a show goin' on.'

There was too much excitement for an immediate letdown. Dan escorted Nevada to the dressing tent where she changed, and when she reappeared he could hardly realize that this girl dressed in skirt and blouse was the shining creature of the arena. They walked back to the tent, and as they walked Nevada spoke warningly.

'We've got a show stopper, Dan. We rolled them off the seats. Let me talk to Tom. I know what we're worth and I'll make him pay it.'

Dan did not know why, but he had taken Nevada's arm when she came out of the tent. He wanted to have something tangible, something to reassure him that all this was real. 'You do whatever you want, Nevada,' he said. 'Whatever you say goes. Gosh! You're the whole act. I'm just along.'

'We're partners,' Nevada refuted firmly. 'We split fifty-fifty. The act wouldn't be anything without us both. But you let me talk to Tom.'

Back at the big top they held a little court, performers entering or coming off, stopping to speak to them and congratulate them. Penny, her act with Purrington finished, paused before them.

'It was swell, Nevada. You and Dan have a swell act.'

'Thanks, Penny.'

'Thanks a lot, Penny,' Dan echoed.

After the performance there was a party in the cookhouse, the performers gathering without prearrangement. Ruffin, big and bluff and a little boisterous, circulated through the crowd, and Fred Kerr, the bookkeeper, talked to a ticket man, cannily transforming the new act into dollars and cents at the ticket window. The Darnells were there, and Captain Purrington and Penny, Bob White and Shorty and Red Halsey, all the show people. Finally the party broke up, leaving the lot in a body to return to the train. Dan did not leave Nevada's side for a moment. Those who occupied the married couples' car passed the two, smiling, still voicing congratulations and good nights, and Nevada, mounting car steps, smiled down at Dan. Then the last of the show people had gone into their cars, and lights glowed all along the side of the train.

'Well, Nevada,' Dan said reluctantly, 'I guess I'd better go.'

Impulsively the girl descended to the ground again. 'It's hard to believe, isn't it, Danny?' she asked. 'You don't think it's real, do you?'

'I never have,' Dan answered.

'In a year or two it will be an old story,' Nevada predicted. 'I wonder how you'll feel then. I wonder if you'll be like all the rest.'

'How do you mean?'

'They were nice enough tonight. They told

us how good we were and what a swell act we had, and every one of them was waiting until they got away from us so that they could pick the act to pieces. Don't ever be that way, Dan.'

Dan laughed. 'I don't think I will be,' he said.

Nevada looked up at him. 'No,' she said slowly, 'I don't think you will be.'

Silence was broken only by the little noises as all through the cars the men and women talked and made ready for the night. By the steps the light was dim and Nevada's face was pale and upturned. The girl's lips were parted slightly, and in her eyes were tenderness and invitation.

The wine of success ran swift and hot in Dan Mar. Without volition he bent swiftly and kissed the parted lips. Nevada's arms stole up around his neck, and Dan, man animal that he was, held her close against him. For long seconds the tableau held, and then, freeing herself, Nevada laughed tremulously.

'We'd better not do that, Dan.'

'Why not?' Dan demanded.

Nevada averted her eyes. 'Because,' she said, 'you don't really mean it.'

'But I do mean it,' Dan insisted. 'You know I do.' Again his arms went out toward the girl but, lithely as she had eluded the rope in the arena, Nevada avoided him. She ran up the car steps and, pausing on the platform, looked back. 'Tell me tomorrow, Dan,' she said softly,

114

'if you mean it.'

Nevada was gone. Dan stood looking at the empty platform, then slowly walked toward his own car. For the instant of their kiss he had loved Nevada Warren, wanted her; his arms had been fierce and his lips insistent. He shook his head as he mounted the steps of his own car.

Two cars away Penny emerged from the shadows beside the train and hurried to her car. Beside the car, in its shadow, Penny had waited until she had gained control of herself before she went in to meet Ruth, to listen to Ruth's comments concerning the new act, to hear Ruth say, 'They've got a swell act, but ...' Penny had seen it all.

In the morning Nevada and Dan talked with Tom Ruffin. Ruffin was both showman and businessman, and he had a shrewd eye for a dollar.

'Just what do you think it's worth, Tom?' Nevada asked. 'You saw how we went over last night. What's the act worth to you?'

'Yo're selling it,' Ruffin reminded, 'Yo're the ones to name the price. What do you think, Dan?'

Nevada glanced warningly at her partner, and Dan remained silent. 'We'll let you have it cheap,' the girl said, turning to Ruffin. 'How about a hundred?'

'A month?' Ruffin asked, his eyes narrowed. 'Sure. I can pay that.'

Nevada laughed. 'A week; apiece,' she said

firmly.

'Do you think you've struck a gold mine?' Ruffin demanded. 'You ain't gold-plated, are you? That's eight hundred a month. I won't pay that.'

'Then what will you pay?'

'I'll pay five hundred.'

Nevada laughed again. 'I know people who would pay that much for the horses,' she scoffed. 'Come again, Tom.'

Dan stood by while the bargaining went back and forth. Nevada came down a trifle; Ruffin went up. A hundred dollars separated the figures.

'I'll split it with you,' Ruffin announced. 'Six-fifty.'

Nevada nodded. 'For the balance of the season,' she agreed, 'and you're to furnish transportation, food, and a new costume for Dan.'

'Are you sure yore name don't begin with Mac?' Ruffin growled good-humoredly. 'All right. I'll do it an' take an option on the act for next year.'

'You'll get no option,' Nevada contradicted. 'Next year the act will cost you a flat thousand dollars. I know where we can get that for it.'

'Maybe,' Ruffin answered skeptically. 'All right. I'll leave out the option clause. I'll make a new contract an' tear up yore old ones.

'You know,' he continued as Nevada read the contract, 'I don't really have to do this. I've got you both under contract an' I could hold you.'

'But not as an act,' Nevada reminded, and signed her name.

'I'll stand you kids a feed in town,' Ruffin said, expansive now that the business was concluded. 'Come on.'

They took a hack from the depot and rode toward the center of the town. Ruffin asked the cabdriver for the name of the best hotel and, when answered, said: 'Stop about two blocks away, will you, bud?'

The driver obliged, and Ruffin helped Nevada to the sidewalk. With the girl between them the men strolled down the street, their appearance attracting attention and comment. Ruffin and Dan were dressed in show clothes: big hats, gaudy shirts, narrow-legged trousers, and boots. Nevada, too, wore a costume and, like the others, a big hat.

'Good advertising,' Ruffin rumbled. 'Maybe they won't read the four sheets but they sure see us.'

Nevada chuckled. '"Always rib the suckers,"' she quoted.

'Ruffin's Wild West is the best in the world,' Ruffin stated complacently.

In the hotel Ruffin said, 'Hang around the lobby for a minute, will you? I'll be right back.' Leaving his guests, he went to the desk. Nevada tucked her hand under Dan's arm.

'More advertising,' she drawled. 'Tom's like

117

a kid; he always toots his horn. Let's sit down and wait for him.'

'Sure,' Dan agreed diffidently.

Nevada led the way. Passing the chairs and lounges in the center of the lobby, they sat down in the deserted writing room. For a while there was a constrained silence between them. They had not been alone together for an instant since the night before. 'Last night, Nevada,' Dan said awkwardly, 'I...'

The girl faced him. 'And what about last night, Dan?' she asked softly.

Dan, looking into Nevada's eyes, did not immediately answer. Nevada spoke again.

'We were both excited last night. We'd put on an act and it had gone over. Is that what you want to tell me, Dan?'

Dan could not bear to see the hurt and the resignation behind those dark eyes. 'No!' he said impulsively. 'That wasn't what I wanted to tell you. I meant what I said last night, an' what I did!'

The pain and the resignation were gone. Nevada's hand fell lightly upon Dan's own where it rested on the arm of his chair. 'Dan...' she began.

'There you are!' Ruffin's voice boomed. 'Say, that's swell. That's all right, that is. When's it goin' to happen?'

Nevada smiled at Dan and answered, 'We haven't gone that far yet, Tom. Not for a while, anyway.'

'Well, by gosh!' Ruffin exclaimed. 'You wait till I spread this around the show. Kind of put one over on me, didn't you? I thought you were practicin' yore act all the time, an' here you were courtin'. Dan, you rascal, I ought to shoot you, takin' my best girl like this!' There was heartiness in Ruffin's voice, but Nevada sensed that the man was driving himself.

'Please, Tom,' she said, 'don't tell anyone, will you? Promise? Dan and I want to keep it to ourselves awhile.'

'Sure ... sure ... you bet!' Reaching down, Ruffin possessed himself of Nevada's hands and drew her to her feet. 'Whatever you say. But you can't keep me from drinkin' a toast to you two kids.'

In the dining room of the hotel Ruffin seated Nevada and then took his own chair. Dan, awkward in unaccustomed grandeur and frightened by the swift turn of events, had little to say. Ruffin did the talking, keeping up a running fire of comment. He ordered champagne and lifted his glass, first to Nevada, then to Dan.

While they waited for dessert a bellboy entered the dining room, circulating unobtrusively among the tables. 'Mr. Ruffin!' he called. 'Mr. Tom Ruffin!'

'Here, boy!' Ruffin removed the napkin from his lap and pushed back his chair. 'Who wants me?'

'There's two gentlemen at the desk, sir.'

119

'You'll excuse me, Nevada? . . . Dan?' Ruffin got up. 'I'll be right back.'

He moved off between the tables, a striking, attention-inspiring figure. Nevada laughed softly.

'I'll bet,' she said, 'that he had himself paged. It would be just like him!'

The desserts came, but Ruffin did not return. Presently the same bellboy came to the table. 'Mr. Ruffin says will you excuse him please? He has some business.'

'I lose my bet,' Nevada laughed. 'We might as well eat this. Tom won't be back.'

*　　　*　　　*

When Ruffin left the table he was glad for the interruption. He had been talking under pressure, forcing joviality under strain. The effort was almost more than he could muster to look at Nevada and see the happiness in her eyes, to glance at Dan Mar and recognize in the clean-cut youngster the things that he himself did not possess. He left the dining room, and as he crossed the lobby to the desk two men stepped out.

'Mr. Ruffin?' one asked.

'I'm Tom Ruffin.'

The speaker held out his hand. 'I'm Bardwell,' he announced. 'I'm chief of police here. This is Mr. Garza, Mr. Ruffin.'

Ruffin shook hands with both men, his eyes

wary. Tom Ruffin had spent a long time in the show business; he had listened to and cared for many a complaint. 'Well, gentlemen?' he asked.

'Let's go in here where we can talk.' Bardwell nodded toward the writing room.

'I've some guests in the dining room,' Ruffin demurred. 'I'd like...'

'Can't you send them word that you'll be busy for a while?' Bardwell asked.

Ruffin beckoned to a bellboy. 'Here, son,' he ordered. 'You got to my table an' tell the folks there I'll not be back. An' here'—he reached into his pocket—'pay the check an' tip the waiter. You can keep the bellboy change.'

'Thank *you*, sir,' the bellboy said, glancing at the crisp bills in his hand. 'Yes sir. Right away!'

In the writing room Ruffin looked questioningly from one to the other of his companions. 'Well,' he said, 'what's the beef, gentlemen? What do you want?'

Bardwell chuckled, but Garza answered quietly: 'There's no "beef," as you call it, Mr. Ruffin. I'm with the Pinkerton Agency, and I asked Mr. Bardwell to come with me when I talked with you.'

'A Pinkerton man?' Ruffin asked slowly. 'Why are you interested in me?'

'We're not particularly interested in you,' Garza answered, 'but we are interested in your show. Before I go any further I'd like to show you my credentials and some newspaper clippings.' He produced an envelope from the inside pocket of his coat and passed it over.

Having glanced at the letter the envelope contained, Ruffin spread the clippings fanlike in his hand. The first was from an Omaha paper and the others, following in dated sequence, from various other newspapers. Each clipping told of some crime of violence, robbery, and one told of murder. Glancing up at the two men who silently watched him, Ruffin asked a question. 'What have these got to do with me?'

Garza took the clippings and the letter, refolding them carefully. 'Nothing with you personally, Mr. Ruffin,' he answered, 'and perhaps nothing with your show. My agency has been employed by an express company. The office of that company was robbed while your show played in town.'

Ruffin sat up alertly. 'You think ...?' he began.

'Every one of those clippings comes from a town where your show played at the time the crime was committed.' Garza replaced the clippings in the envelope. 'We think that there's a connection, Mr. Ruffin. Now wait a minute!' His upraised hand stopped the words that Ruffin had ready. 'We're accusing no one, but we can't overlook so definite a clue. Mr. Pinkerton himself assigned me to this job. We aren't accusing you at all, but we think that your show has been victimized by a gang of toughs. It wouldn't be the first time that has happened, would it, Bardwell?'

The police chief laughed sharply. 'Not by a long shot,' he said. 'Half the shows and carnivals that come to town are crooked.'

'I run a Sunday-school outfit,' Ruffin rasped. 'There's no grifters with my show, you know that, Bardwell. There's no dips or yeggs or con men in my outfit!'

'We know that you run a clean show,' Garza assured placidly. 'I've made it a point to learn that. That's why we came to you. I knew I could count on your co-operation.'

Ruffin, somewhat mollified, leaned back. 'What do you want to do?' he asked.

'Naturally,' Garza said pleasantly, 'you can't know the background of every man you hire. I want to travel with you, Mr. Ruffin. I may not find a thing, and then again I may.'

'Why, sure,' Ruffin said. 'I'll take you along. You can have a place in the car an'...'

He stopped, for Garza was shaking his head. 'I want your boss canvasman to hire me,' Garza said. 'When you meet me on the lot you won't know me and I won't know you. I spent a little time in the show business, and I don't think I'll have any trouble doing the work.' The detective laughed reminiscently. 'I'll make you a good canvasman. All that I want you to do is to see that there's a place for me. Tell your boss canvasman that he needs another man. I'll be on hand to get the job.'

'I'll tell him to hire you,' Ruffin agreed.

'No. Just tell him to take on another man, that's all. I'll be at the lot tonight, Mr. Ruffin.'

CHAPTER NINE

The fair date was a three days' stand, and on the morning of the last day Dan got up early. He dressed quietly and, stepping out on the platform, saw the sun, barely risen. As the cinders crunched beneath his boots he grinned at the sun and pulled in a deep breath of the clean-swept morning air. Striding along toward the town, he thought that it had been quite some time since he had last seen the sun rise. Like the rest of the show people, he had acquired the habit of taking time off the first of the day and adding it to the other end. It was a queer business, this show business; its values were different from any other, its time was different. Last night, for instance, Nevada, in the entry after their exit, had frowned as she listened to the applause, and she and Dan took only two bows.

'Not so good tonight,' Nevada had commented. 'They didn't like us as well as they did this afternoon.' It was odd that a man's livelihood should depend upon the popularity of an act, the amount of applause that it received.

A little restaurant beckoned Dan, and he entered for a cup of coffee. When he left the restaurant the town was coming to life. Dan walked on toward the show grounds, passing a few people on the street, aware of their curious eyes. When he reached the lot he found activity. The performers might sleep late, but the hostlers were up and busy. Dan entered the stock tent where horses munched grain and men were busy with manure forks and a cart. The stock tent, Dan thought, was a big traveling livery barn. He strolled along the aisle, glancing at the glistening, sleek-haired rumps. Domino turned and looked at him, and Nigger flipped an ear before returning to his oats.

A passing hostler grinned at Dan and spoke. 'Look pretty good, don't they?'

'They sure do,' Dan agreed.

Leaving the stock tent, he wandered on across the lot toward the fairgrounds. Here, too, was activity. As though drawn by a magnet, Dan sought the livestock pavilion. Bales of hay flanked the stalls and grain sacks were staked against the hay. Exhibitors were grooming their animals, getting them in shape for the day, and Dan, stopping behind a stall, looked at the broad red backs of the cattle in the enclosure. Here was beef on the hoof. A cow turned a placid white face toward him, stared incuriously, and went on eating; and its exhibitor, a brown-faced, knotted oldster, came from between the animals and grinned at Dan.

'Final judgin' today,' he announced. 'They look pretty good, don't they?'

'You bet,' Dan agreed, and glanced down at the ribbons that decorated a bale of straw.

'I won the reserve championship with that bull last year,' the gnarled man informed. 'Won his class with him yesterday. I figure to take top bull in the show. Think I can do it?'

Dan nodded and, hearing a footstep crunching straw beside him, turned to see the prototype of his gnarled acquaintance. The newcomer wore a wide black hat, battered and with the brim rolled at an angle long familiar to Dan Mar. His feet were encased in boots, and a twill shirt and denim overalls occupied the space between hat and boots.

'He wasn't there, Jake,' the man with the hat announced.

Jake grunted. 'We got up too early for him. When will he get here, Pete?'

'There's nobody in the office a-tall,' Pete reported, and glanced at Dan. 'Say, yo're with the show, ain't you?'

Dan nodded.

'Yo're the feller that puts on that ropin' act with the girl?'

'That's right.'

Jake came out of the stall and joined Pete. They were unmistakably brothers. The three men stood in line, squinting at the cattle.

126

'Too fat,' Pete said suddenly. 'Yo're goin' to have to take some of that off, Jake. I cain't use 'em this way.' He glanced at Dan. 'I want them bulls to have on their workin' clothes before I take 'em home.'

Dan had been thinking the same thing. Admiring the animals, he had nevertheless faulted them. The bulls were too fat to turn out. Put on the range, they would get sore-footed and lie around the water holes, not attending to business as they should.

'Where's home?' Dan asked suddenly. 'Oklahomy.'

Apparently Dan's face asked a question, for Pete continued: 'Jake an' me's got a pardnership. He raises bulls an' feeds cattle. I raise the cattle.'

'Oh,' Dan said.

'You know anythin' about cows?' Pete stared at Dan.

A little spot of irritation rose in Dan. Did he know anything about cows! 'I was raised with 'em,' he answered.

'I couldn't tell.' Pete's voice was apologetic. 'Sometimes you show fellers wear the clothes but don't have the *sabe*.'

'We've got a place up North,' Dan said unthinkingly. 'We've got some Herefords.'

The gnarled face beside him brightened. 'Where do you get yore bulls?' Jake asked.

'In Nebraska. From Arning and Porter.'

Both men nodded. 'They got some good

127

stock,' Jake said. 'We went up there to look at 'em one time. Remember, Pete?'

'Sure I remember.' Pete was looking up the alley toward the pavilion entrance. 'That secretary just come in. Want me to see him?'

'I'll go,' Jake answered, and strode off. Pete squatted on his boot heels against the straw bales. 'Got a little trouble gettin' a heifer classed right,' he drawled. 'She's a long yearlin', an' they want to put her in the two-year-old class. Jake'll 'tend to it.'

Dan nodded, and Pete eyed him quizzically. 'That's a right nice circus you got,' Pete praised. 'Pretty good show. I'd like it better if you had some elephants an' lions an' such, but this'll do.'

'We don't carry a menagerie with a Wild West show,' Dan said.

'No, I reckon not.' Pete selected a straw and chewed it. 'How come yo're with a circus if you got a ranch?'

'Why ...' Dan said, 'it's a good job. There's money in it.'

'Money in cows too.' Pete rolled the straw. 'I'd ruther foller a cow than get up an' make a show of myself. There's sense to follerin' cattle.'

'And no sense in the show business?' Dan laughed.

'No.' The straw was spat out. 'Just gettin' up in front of a bunch of folks an' doin' things that don't never happen. No offense, mister.'

'How do you mean they never happen?'

Pete's gnarled face twisted further in thought. 'Well,' he said, 'f'instance, I ain't never roped no girl in tights down on my place. I ain't never seen one. When I rope, it's at somethin' I want to ketch because I need it. Yo're a right pretty roper, though,' The addition was hastily made.

Jake joined them again. 'You'd better come up there, Pete,' he announced. 'That secretary feller won't believe me.'

Pete got up and glanced apologetically at Dan. 'All right,' he said. 'I liked yore show right good, mister. It's all right for a show. Come down an' see me sometime.' Pete followed his brother along the alley.

'Come down an' see me sometime.' Dan grinned. He hadn't heard that for months. In Brule a cowman from Montana might say 'come an' see me sometime' to a man from Colorado and mean it. The old neighborliness that took no account of distance, the tight clannishness of the cowman; suddenly Dan realized that he had missed it, did miss it. He looked at the cattle again and then walked slowly along the stalls.

When Dan left the livestock pavilion he saw Penny Thwaite going into the building that housed the grain exhibits. Impulsively he followed her, finding her standing in front of a giant display of fruit and grain.

'Out pretty early,' Dan greeted as he

stopped. 'I didn't expect to see you in here, Penny.'

The girl turned, her face flushed. 'I always go to see the exhibits when we play a fair,' she said. 'You're out pretty early yourself, Dan.'

'I went over to look at the stock. Have you seen them yet?'

Penny shook her head. 'I save that until last,' she answered. 'I always look at the grain first, and then at the canning and the sewing exhibits, and then see the livestock.'

'That sounds like a good program.' Dan grinned at the girl. 'Mind if I go along? Or would you rather I didn't?'

'Come along if you want to.'

As the constraint wore off, Dan and Penny enjoyed themselves. They looked at the grain and the fruit and, in the homemaker's building, at quilts and lace and cans of pickles and preserves and jellies and jams. In the livestock pavilion they saw the cattle, the horses, the hogs, and the sheep.

It was almost noon when the tour was finished and Dan and Penny left the Pavilion, talking and laughing freely.

'Remember when we went to the fair at Spruce Hill?' Dan asked as they walked toward the exit. 'We rode the Ferris wheel and I bought you a hot dog and you got too much mustard on it.'

'And burned my mouth, and you bought me pop to put out the fire!' Penny laughed. 'We used to have some good times together, didn't we?'

'Yeah. We did.' Dan caught the spirit of the talk. 'You were sure an ornery little devil. I remember the first time I went to your ranch with Dad. They were roundin' up, an' they left me to look after you. You ran off, remember?'

'And you found me,' Penny laughed up at Dan. 'Away over in the Vinegar Creek roughs.'

'An' we played outlaw an' sheriff the rest of the day.' Dan chuckled in recollection. 'That was sure a good country to hide in. I've always thought that if I ever had to go on the dodge I'd head right back for that place. Remember how we killed the rabbit and you cooked it?'

'It was half raw and we didn't have any salt!' Penny made a grimace of distaste. 'We used to have some good times, you and Carl and I. Carl ...' She stopped. The mention of her brother's name had been unthinking, and it came like a dash of cold water to quench their merriment.

'Penny,' Dan said slowly, 'I wish ...'

'What do you wish, Dan?'

'I wish that you'd teamed up with me when you came back to the show.'

'But you've got a good act. You and Nevada have a better act than you and I could ever have. I can't ride like she can.'

'Maybe you're right,' Dan agreed. 'But I didn't like having you work with Smokey.'

'I'm not working with him now,' Penny

131

reminded.

'Why did you quit Smokey?' Dan asked abruptly. 'Did he try to get funny with you?'

Penny would not lie, but she would equivocate. 'Captain Purrington needed something to dress up his act,' she answered. 'I used to work with him at winter quarters, and he thought it would be a good thing to have a girl assistant.'

'It wasn't on account of Smokey?'

'I've told you. The captain hired me.'

It seemed to Penny that Dan's eyes bored through her and her subterfuge. 'Somebody told me,' Dan drawled, 'that Smokey was carryin' a gun for me. Is that right, Penny?'

'He does carry a gun Dan.' Alarm crept into Penny's voice. 'You won't have any trouble with Smokey, will you? Please, Dan.'

'I told Tom Ruffin that I'd lay off Darnell as long as he laid off me.' The man's voice was iron-hard. 'I'll do that, but if he gets funny with you I'll ...' Dan paused. 'I wish you hadn't joined the show,' he completed. 'Sometimes I wish I never had. If Carl...'

'You still blame yourself about Carl, don't you, Dan?' Penny said softly.

The man nodded soberly.

'Please don't.' Penny's voice was smaller still.

They walked on in silence for a time, then: 'Penny,' Dan said, 'I got all of Carl's tack, didn't I? Spurs an' all?'

'Why, yes.' Penny stopped, and, perforce, Dan halted. 'He had two pairs of spurs. Didn't you get both pairs? I had them listed.'

'I got them both,' Dan answered. 'I just wanted to know if he had more than the two sets.'

'No.' Penny resumed walking. 'Is there something wrong with the spurs? If there is, I'll take them back and pay you for them.'

'They're all right,' Dan answered abstractedly.

When they reached the lot Dan and Penny separated. Dan, seeking the pad room, opened his chest and looked at the spurs again. Once more he tried a rowel against the spur tracks on the saddle and then, dropping the spurs back into the chest, closed the lid.

Captain Purrington saw Dan and Penny come on the lot together and separate. The captain had been looking for Penny, having a matter pertaining to the act to discuss with her. Penny went into the prop tent, and Purrington, leaving the stock tent, hurried to catch her. As he neared the tent a small man, inclined to plumpness, came out. The two men met and Purrington halted. 'Garza!' he exclaimed.

The roustabout did not change expression. 'You don't know me,' he said swiftly. 'Remember that, Purrington. You don't know me.'

'But what are you doing with the show?'

Garza looked casually around the lot. There

was no one within hearing distance, and he smiled at the captain. 'Working,' he answered. 'I knew you were with this show. I tried to see you last night but I couldn't find you.'

'I went to the train right after the show,' Purrington explained. 'You're working? You haven't ...?'

'I'm still with Pinkerton. I'm on a case.'

'With Ruffin's show?'

Garza nodded vigorously. 'Right now I'm running an errand for Brannigan,' he said. 'I haven't time to talk. When can I see you?'

The captain's eyes narrowed in thought. 'After the performance?' he asked. 'Can you get downtown?'

'I'll meet you by the corner of the First National,' Garza said. 'At half-past six. Right?'

'Right,' Purrington answered. 'I'll be there.'

The detective hurried away, and Purrington, his business with Penny forgotten, turned and walked back toward the stock tent.

At half-past six that evening Purrington was on the bank corner. Garza, a few minutes late, came up and nodded his greeting. He still wore the rough clothing of a roustabout and he spoke swiftly. 'We don't want to attract attention, Purrington. There are some other show people downtown. Follow me, but take your time.' Garza went on, and the captain, strolling, occasionally looking into a store window, followed.

134

The small man led the way toward the streets near the railroad tracks. Here, where cheap hotels, restaurants, and saloons mingled their signs with those of pawnshops and clothing stores, Garza chose an entrance. Purrington, having waited a few minutes, followed Garza. The sign above the entrance told of a hotel upstairs, and in the hallway Garza said: 'I've got a room. Come on.'

There was no clerk at the dingy desk on the second floor, and Garza led the way along a hall, opened a door, and gestured the captain into a room. Locking the door, the detective tossed his hat on the bed and smiled at his companion. 'I haven't seen you since Ashleyville. That's been ... it's been eight years.'

Purrington nodded. 'I left there after that thing was wound up,' he said. 'Resigned my commission in the Rangers and quit.'

'And since then?'

'I traveled for a cartridge company for a while. Then got into the show business.'

Garza sat down beside his hat. 'I need some help, Purrington,' he said. 'I want you to give me a hand.'

'With what?' The captain frowned.

Garza brought out his envelope. 'It's in here,' he answered.

Captain Purrington scanned the clippings carefully. 'So?' he said, looking up.

'You saw the dates. Every job was done

while Ruffin's show played the town or a near-by town. They're traveling with the show.'

'They might be.' The captain tapped the envelope against his palm.

'Almost for a certainty.' Garza seemed positive. 'I talked to Ruffin and tied up with the show. You've got some tough boys in your canvas crew, Captain.'

'You don't find angels raising canvas,' Purrington commented.

'No, you don't. I didn't tell Ruffin all of it. A street-railway collector was killed. He had a mask in his hand when they found him. Must have pulled it off one of the men who killed him.'

'Murder too?' Purrington's eyes were narrow.

'Murder.' Garza nodded. 'You can help a lot if you will.'

It seemed that Purrington debated with himself. 'I quit the business once,' he said. 'I ... What do you want me to do?'

'Keep your eyes open ... and I want to know where the mask came from. Are masks used in the show?'

'In the stage holdup.'

Garza nodded his gratification. 'I'll get a look at them,' he said. 'Well, Captain? Will you?'

Purrington nodded slowly. 'I can't turn you down, and you know it,' he growled. 'Not after

Ashleyville. How will I get to see you, Garza?'

'I'll be on the lot. Give me a little time to fit into things. I'll get a job in the property tent if I can, and when you've got something for me you can tip me off. I'll get to you all right.'

Purrington got up. 'I hate it on Tom's account,' he said. 'Do me a favor, Garza. If you get things lined up, try to keep Ruffin out of it. It's bad advertising.'

'Sure thing, Captain,' Garza agreed. 'I'll keep Ruffin out of it if I can. We'll handle it so that the show won't be mentioned.'

CHAPTER TEN

The men Garza worked with did not at first accept the new roustabout. They called him 'Fatso,' laughed at him because his hands were soft and bore no calluses, and rode him unmercifully. Garza, for all his plumpness, packed hard muscles and an ability to use them, but for a time he stood the riding. He found, within hours after he was hired, that there were cliques and castes among the laborers just as there were among the performers. The hostlers looked down on the canvas crew and these in turn looked down upon the hostlers.

But, having joined the show, Garza set about the next step in his plan. By being always

137

available and always cheerful he ingratiated himself with Brannigan, and after a week of hard work with the canvasmen, a week in which his hands blistered to tatters and then slowly began to heal, he was helping in the property tent. Garza almost shouted with delight when he examined the masks used in the stage robbery and discovered that they were identical with the one found in the hand of the murdered street-railway collector.

Now a stroke of fortune descended upon Garza. Marking one of the masks for future identification, he hid it in his battered telescope grip.

The loss of the mask made Branningan swear. 'We're always losin' 'em,' the prop boss growled. 'You go over to Mary Flarity, Fatso, an' tell her we've got to have another mask.'

Garza went on the errand gladly and found Mrs. Flarity at her perpetual work. There was always something for the wardrobe mistress to do, and her machine was humming when Garza entered and stated his errand.

'Another mask, is it?' the wardrobe mistress rasped. 'An' who has lost his this time? That Dan Mar, I suppose. If it's him again, he can just do without an' use a bandanny.'

Mrs. Flarity made the mask, and Garza took it to Brannigan. 'She was cussing Mar,' he reported. 'Said that he was always losing masks.'

'He didn't lose this one,' Brannigan assured.

'He's not with the spec.'

'Did Mar used to work the stage robbery?' Garza asked innocently.

'Sure,' Brannigan answered. 'He worked at everythin' before he got this new act with Nevada, the lucky stiff!'

More judicious priming and some subtle pumping told Garza what he wished to know. Dan Mar had worked in the stagecoach spectacle about the time of the collector's murder. Garza went just so far. He did not learn that Dan had been in the spectacle for only a day.

Because of his new knowledge Garza devoted what time he could to watching Dan. He saw nothing suspicious and finally sought Captain Purrington in his car. Garza had finally come to the point where he needed help.

The captain had been reading and marked his place with his finger as he let Garza in. When the door was closed and both were seated Purrington asked: 'What luck?'

Garza never completely trusted anyone. He shrugged. 'Not much so far. Have you seen anything?'

'Nothing out of the way.' Purrington put down his book. 'I've been watching the papers.'

'And so have I. They're quiet for the present. I'd like to go over some things with you, Captain. I've noticed that the performers are pretty friendly with the roustabouts.'

'Why, no more than usual,' Purrington said. 'I hadn't noticed that. I thought that they stayed pretty well to themselves.'

'I've seen some things.' Garza took one of the captain's cigars. 'This Darnell, for instance. I've seen him in the prop tent more than once. Mar too. What about Mar, Captain?'

'Dan?' Purrington laughed. 'The last person in the world to suspect, Garza. He comes from a ranch next to Ruffin's place up North. Just a kid, and this is the first time he's ever been away from home.'

'You like him pretty well?'

'He's a good boy. Green as grass, of course, but a good honest boy. He's making quite a success in the show.'

'Yeah.' Garza's face told nothing. 'I caught his act. He's good. The girl's got him outclassed, though.'

'Nevada's been in the show business all her life.'

'Are they kind of sweet on each other?'

Purrington frowned. He had noticed that Dan spent a great deal of time with Nevada and, because of Penny, was concerned. 'I don't know,' he answered slowly. 'There's a girl from up North that thinks Dan is pretty nice, but recently he's been with Nevada a lot. That's natural, of course.'

'Yeah. Because of the act. How about Mar? Has he got expensive tastes? Does he spend a lot of money?'

'No,' Purrington said, and then frowned at his companion. 'See here, Garza, if you suspect Dan Mar, you're barking up the wrong tree. Dan's no more capable of being mixed up in a thing like this than I am. Why, he was in the bank at Brule when it was robbed. They made him lie down on the floor and afterwards locked him in the vault.'

Garza's face showed no expression, but mentally he added a tally. He knew that often banks were scouted by others than those who did the actual work of robber.

'How about the girl? Nevada, I mean. Does she spend much money?'

'Quite a lot,' Purrington answered. 'But she makes good money. I tell you, Garza, you're looking at the wrong man. Dan's not in this.'

Garza shrugged. He had intended to ask the captain to keep an eye on Dan Mar. Now he saw that his friend would not do for the task. Purrington liked Dan too well.

'How about Darnell?' the detective queried.

'Now there,' Purrington said slowly, 'is another horse. Smokey Darnell spends a lot of money, and he's crooked as a dog's hind leg. I happen to know of a thing he got into a while back.' The captain scowled.

'What was it?'

'Woman trouble,' Purrington said shortly. 'But it will pay you to watch Smokey.'

Garza asked questions about others of the

141

performers, and Purrington's answers were succinct and clear. Presently the detective left. As he crossed to the door he paused beside the medal case.

'Quite a display you've got,' he commented.

Purrington joined him. 'Most of them I got when I worked for UMC,' he answered. 'I don't know why I keep them.'

Garza nodded toward the little gold saddle. 'That's no medal for shooting,' he observed.

Purrington detached the miniature saddle from the board. 'Ruffin gave that one to me,' he said. 'He had four of them made in Mexico, one for himself, one for Darnell, and the others for Carl Thwaite and me. See? My name's on the back of it.'

Garza examined the saddle closely. 'A beautiful thing,' he commented. 'I'd like to have one.'

'There's not much chance of your getting one just like this,' Purrington laughed. 'I wouldn't part with mine, and I don't think Ruffin or Darnell would give theirs away. Penny gave Carl's saddle to Dan Mar, and I know he means to keep it.'

'Well,' Garza said briskly, returning the saddle to the case, 'I've got to go, Captain. So long.' He left the car not at all satisfied. He had hoped to get more information from Purrington concerning Dan Mar and had intended to exact the captain's promise to watch Dan for him. Now Dan's surveillance must be added to his own tasks. Friendships and preconceived ideas were always balling things up in his business, Garza thought.

The Pinkerton man was not alone in that opinion. Dan, too, was finding that friendships complicated things. He was filled with curiosity concerning two matters: why Penny had quit working with the Darnells and gone to work with Captain Purrington, and the source of the spur tracks across Carl's saddle. About the latter there was little he could do. The tracks had been made on Ruffin's ranch and only a few of the people who were on the ranch at the time of Carl's death were with the show. Covertly Dan examined the spurs that these men wore and found exactly nothing. Naturally he could not go to them and say: 'Let me see your spurs. I want to find out if they fit a set of tracks across my saddle.' He was forced to limit his investigation to a scrutiny of the spurs as they were worn, and he saw none that had a prong missing from their rowels.

Nor was he any more successful in discovering why Penny had quit the Darnell act. Purrington, cautiously approached, told Dan vaguely that he had decided to dress up his act and had persuaded Penny to work with him. Penny had nothing whatever to say on the subject. Indeed, Penny avoided Dan. He would seek her company during such free time as he had, only to find that, very shortly, someone else had joined them or that Penny had business elsewhere.

And Dan had very little free time. It seemed to him that he was continually with Nevada. They worked together in the arena twice a day when the show was set up. When the show traveled Nevada found constant excuse for Dan to visit her in her car. Man that he was, Dan liked Nevada's company, liked the way she smiled at him or touched his arm or fussed over him, but he did not want to be with her all the time. He craved and needed the companionship of other men, and he had but little of it.

Ruffin's Wild West moved inland. Presently it would swing north from the tier of Southern states. The season was more than half over. In October the show would break up, some performers going to their homes in various parts of the country, some to winter quarters at Ruffin's ranch. Dan was weary of the show. Sometimes he thought of the two brothers, Pete and Jake, whom he had encountered at the fair. Pete's words, 'I never seen no girl in tights on my place,' came back to him now and then when he worked in the arena with Nevada. The act began to become standardized, the motions mechanical, smooth as silk. Applause, the two or three bows that he and Nevada took after the act, all of it began to lose its first keen edge. Dan, like Nevada, began to listen to the stamping feet and the clapping hands, measuring them calculatingly.

They meant more money or less money in the white wagon and that was all.

On the first payday after the presentation of the Cowboy and the Lady, Dan counted the bills in his envelope with some awe. Here was more money than many a man received for a year's work back North. Three hundred and twenty-five dollars! Dan counted it again.

Nevada had accompanied him to the white wagon, and her envelope was in her hand. 'What are you going to do with that, Dan?' she asked.

'Pay some bills,' Dan answered. 'I still owe for my tack, an' I want to get that paid for. This one'—he picked up the top bill, a ten-dollar note—'I'm goin' to keep. Someday I'll frame it. That's the first money I ever got for the act, an' I think I'll keep it for luck.'

Nevada laughed. 'You'll spend it before the season's over.'

'I'll just bet you!' Dan scoffed. 'I'm goin' to put it away.' Folding the ten-dollar bill, he tucked it in his shirt pocket. 'Right in the old suitcase.'

'You'd better bank the whole thing,' Nevada advised. 'Money's the easiest thing there is to get rid of, and there are some around the lot that would like to help you spend it.'

'I like to pack it around.' Dan grinned, patting the pocket that contained his bank roll. 'It feels good.'

'And you'll have it stolen,' Nevada

predicted. 'Better bank it, Dan.'

'I'll look after it,' Dan assured, and then, changing the subject: 'Looks like a poor day, doesn't it? Look at the clouds.'

Nevada turned her face toward the sky. The clouds hung, lowering over the show grounds, promising rain and a poor crowd.

'It does look bad,' Nevada agreed. 'Thank the Lord it didn't rain before we got here. It wouldn't be so good working in mud.'

'We've been lucky so far,' Dan stated. 'Well, we've got our money. Let's go.'

They worked before a small crowd that afternoon, only a few people braving the threatening rain to see the show. There were spasmodic showers, and the back yard became a morass. Performers passing between pad room and big top, traveling from stock tent to dressing tent, wore slickers and covered their boots with overshoes. The roustabouts made the best of it. Some of them had raincoats and some wore boots as they sloshed about in the mud, loosening guy ropes and otherwise seeing that the tents were properly attended. Horses coming into the arena brought mud on their hoofs, and there was a slippery spot or two. Once during the performance Nigger struck a bad place, slid, and caused Dan to miss his loop.

The rain dampened the spirits of the performers. They were surly and short-spoken when they finished the performance. The train stood on a siding half a mile from the grounds, and many of the show people, rather than walk to the cars through the rain, stayed on the lot, uncomfortable and cold.

At the night performance matters were even worse. With nightfall the rain began in earnest, a steady downpour accompanied by wind that billowed the canvas of the big top. Only a handful of people came out for the show, and the performance was not up to par.

Nevada spoke to Dan as they waited in the entry. 'You were short with your loop when I did that back flip. Watch it tonight!'

'Nigger slipped,' Dan apologized. 'I'm sorry, Nevada.'

Suddenly the girl smiled. 'Rain gets show people,' she said. 'You know that. You've seen it happen before. I'm sorry I was so short with you.'

'That's all right,' Dan answered. 'Look, Nevada, let's go in an' put on a real show. The customers ought to get their money back on what they've seen so far.'

Nevada's hand touched Dan's. 'That's what I like about you,' she answered. 'You're real show people. All right, we'll give them a run for their money.'

Dan was as good as his word, and Nevada equaled him. The act went smoothly, flashingly, from beginning to conclusion, and, as though they were ashamed and wanted to extenuate their laxity, those that followed Dan and Nevada worked as hard as though the big top were filled. Even Ruffin caught the spirit of the thing and made his announcements ring in the almost empty tent.

The good performance raised spirits. When the show was over the performers gathered in the cookhouse, besieging the cook for a snack. They drank coffee and talked and laughed and joked while overhead the rain beat down steadily on the canvas. Before the party broke up Ruffin appeared.

'I've got hacks for you folks,' he announced. 'Come on. Ladies first!' The women piled into the three vehicles, laughing and giggling. 'No more room,' Ruffin finally called. 'I'll be back as soon as I unload the girls.' He climbed up beside a driver and the hacks rolled away.

Dan pulled his slicker across his shoulders. There were more men than women with the show, and three cabs could not possibly carry all of them. 'I'm goin' to walk,' he announced. 'Ruffin can't take us all anyhow. Comin', Red?'

Red shook his head. 'I'm goin' to drink another cup of coffee,' he answered. 'Any time the boss hires a hack I'll ride in it. I'll wait till he gets back an' see if there's room enough.'

'Yo're goin' to get wet, Dan!' Bob White prophesied.

'I won't melt if I do,' Dan retorted. 'All right, you lilies, if you're afraid of gettin' wet, stay here. It's stopped rainin' anyhow.' Buckling

148

the slicker, Dan stepped out into the lessening downpour.

He left the cookhouse and, crossing beside the big top, heard the canvas slat and rattle in the wind. The rain came on again, stronger than before, and for an instant he was tempted to turn back. Then, thinking of the roasting he would receive should he return to the cookhouse, Dan ducked his head into the wind and plowed ahead.

Water dripped from his hatbrim, running down in a steady stream. Mud sucked at his overshoes, but he plodded on steadily, his progress further hampered by the wind that whipped his slicker against his legs.

Some two blocks beyond the show ground Dan was thankful to reach a board sidewalk, but the boards, wet with rain, combined with the mud on his overshoes to make him slip and almost fall. Dan righted himself, angry because he had left the shelter of the cookhouse. He was just a plain fool, he thought as he scraped mud off against the edge of the walk. Someday he would learn. Resuming progress, he passed the dark dwellings that were scattered on either side of the walk. It was, Dan thought, dark as the inside of a black cow. Ahead of him, dim and misted by the rain, a single street light glowed. Dan marked progress by that light, twice losing the sidewalk and stepping off into the mud. At the light he paused a moment and then resumed his journey. Rain and night again closed down upon him, and he glanced back to orient himself. Black bodies loomed against the light. Dan saw an upraised arm. A voice snarled, 'Take him! Damn you! Take ...' A blow crashed down against Dan's sodden hat, battering it against his head, stunning him, and the treacherous, wet, slippery sidewalk betrayed him. He went down, and as he fell a knife ripped through his slicker, cutting his arm and parting the stiff yellow oilcloth like so much air.

CHAPTER ELEVEN

The knife scratch acted as a spur caught in the shoulder of a bucker. Dan humped under the slicker, finishing the business that the knife had begun. Already cut from shoulder to hem, the oilcloth parted at the collar and hung open. As Dan scrambled up the slicker dropped away and he was free of its hampering folds. Just in time. The two attackers, one big, one smaller, advanced again.

'Slough him!' the smaller man yelped. 'Tear him down!'

That registered with Dan. The words were familiar enough; he had heard them ever since he joined Ruffin's Wild West. 'Slough it! Tear it down!' So did the boss canvasman command his crew when the tents were to be struck. But

150

Dan had no time to think of the words or ponder on them. He gathered himself, catlike, and plunged in.

In perfect physical condition, muscles like smoothly oiled steel powered by dynamite, Dan did not need to plan an attack or a defense. He had that instinct possessed by natural fighting men which carried him forward into the right place and made him do the right thing when he got there. Better still, he was unhampered by any ethics; he fought naturally, like an animal, with hands and feet and jerking knees. He was, for the instant, a pure savage battling for life, and the very suddenness and ferocity of his attack saved him.

Dan's flying fists found flesh, and bone crunched against bone. His knee, lashing up, caught a man's groin, and that man went down, rolling in the mud. His fingers, talonlike, ripped at cloth and flesh. The slippery footing did not help, and a clublike blow fell on Dan's shoulder, numbing his whole side. His hat was gone, and had that blow found his head, the fight would have been over. Dan's arm dropped limply as he went down, but he lashed out with his feet, staving off the attack. He snarled as he fought, a formless, animal sound, and as his muddy foot found a target a man grunted.

The man who had been kneed in the groin was rising now, still bent double with his pain, and his big companion loomed above Dan. The night was black with rain, and they were blacker figures in it, grim devils who fought, growled, and twisted in the mud, seeking no quarter and giving none. From the direction of the railroad small sparks gleamed yellow through the night and rain, a glowworm procession. Dan lunged up, savagely butting, striking, forcing his attacker back, hardly feeling the blows that rained upon the muscles of his back. And then a man squawled: 'They're comin'. Beat it! Beat it!'

One more blow fell, and then Dan was free. He lunged forward, hit the edge of the sidewalk, and went down. In the street sounded the steady plopping of horses trotting through the mud, and the glowworm resolved itself into the lights of the hacks returning to the show ground. Dan lay panting, and then as the hacks came abreast he struggled to a sitting posture and his voice, hoarse, formless, beat against the rain.

'Hey ... hey there!'

'Whoa!' In the street the hack lights stopped. Dan lurched to his feet. A man rasped: 'Who is it? These hacks are hired. We can't take you.'

Dan slithered through the mud toward the voice. Ruffin said: 'Go on. I've hired these hacks. You can't ...' He broke off. The dim light struck Dan as he placed his one good hand on the muddy wheel to brace himself.

'My good Lord!' Ruffin exclaimed. 'Dan!

What happened to you, boy? Get in here.' And then Ruffin was out in the mud and the rain, helping Dan into the hack.

'Turn around,' Ruffin commanded his driver. 'Take us back to the cars. You two go on to the lot and get the others.'

Ruffin's driver expostulated. 'He's all muddy. He'll get the inside of the hack muddy. Them are new cushions!'

'Get turned around!' Ruffin rasped. He dropped down beside Dan on the seat, slamming the door closed. The hack driver's words were lost as the hack swayed and a cramped wheel scraped against the side when the vehicle turned.

'For God's sake, Dan!' Ruffin's hand caught Dan's injured arm. 'What happened?'

'Easy!' Dan flinched. 'That arm's hurt. I don't know, Tom. All I know is that they jumped me.'

'But what were you doin' walkin'? I told you I'd be back with the hacks.'

'I didn't think there'd be room.' Dan's voice was perceptibly weaker as excitement drained away. 'I started to walk. I'd got part way, an' when I looked back I saw 'em. One of 'em yelled, "Slough him!" an' then they jumped me.'

'Did you see who they were? Did you recognize 'em?'

'No. Let me lean back, Tom. I'm kind of sick.'

'Get yore head down,' Ruffin ordered. 'Here, let me.' He pushed Dan forward, supporting the boy's head with his hand. Dan fought against the nausea.

'One of 'em had a knife,' he muttered. 'Got me in the arm.'

'Just take it easy,' Ruffin soothed. 'We'll be there in a minute.'

The cab stopped beside the train, and the driver and Ruffin helped Dan into the car.

Ruffin snapped orders as he lowered Dan into a chair. 'Get back to the lot an' get hold of Doc. Bring him here as fast as you can. Get gone now!'

The driver went out, and Ruffin, wheeling to Dan, began to unbutton the boy's shirt. Dan half lifted a hand, but Ruffin's gruff 'I'll do it' forestalled the movement.

The shirt came off and was thrown on the floor. Dan's exposed torso showed a great bruise already forming on his shoulder, and on the shoulder and biceps of his left arm was a long, bleeding gash.

'Damn it!' Ruffin swore. 'That will lay you up. You can't work. Ain't that hell?'

Despite his wounds and dizzy head, Dan smiled. That was so like Tom Ruffin to think of events in terms of their effect on the show.

'I've got to tie that up till Doc gets here,' Ruffin growled. 'Here. This will do!' He bound a clean handkerchief around Dan's arm, drawing it tight and tying it; then, stepping

154

back, he surveyed his patient. 'You need a drink,' Ruffin declared. 'I'll get you one. My Lord, Dan, this is a hell of a thing to have happen. It'll ruin your act with Nevada.'

'I'll be all right,' Dan assured. 'I don't feel bad.'

'I'll get you that drink.' Ruffin busied himself at the desk. Dan heard glass clink against glass. He pushed Ruffin's hand away and straightened a trifle.

'Let me,' he ordered.

The whisky burned in his mouth and slid hot and potent down his throat, loosening the cramped knot of his belly and strengthening him. Excited voices sounded outside the car, and feet tramped on steps and platform as the car swayed with added weight. Men came boiling in, the show doctor among the first, and Dan could see Red and Bob White and Captain Purrington and Smokey's dark, saturnine face.

'Stand back now,' the doctor ordered. 'Let me look at him. What happened to you, boy? Did you tangle with a wildcat? Here, somebody get some hot water.'

The doctor was busy as he spoke, untying Ruffin's improvised bandaging.

'How bad is he hurt, Doc?' Ruffin's voice was anxious. 'Will it keep him from workin'?'

'He'll not work for a while,' the physician answered grimly. 'Where's that hot water? Get this crowd out of here, Ruffin. I want room to work.'

'Red, see if you can get some hot water!' Ruffin commanded. 'Now back up, boys. Dan ain't killed. He's goin' to be all right. Cap, you stay here. The rest of you get out.'

The doctor had straightened and was holding Dan's arm, his thumb pressing the cut to check the bleeding. The car swayed again as men moved. 'Open my bag, Captain, and give me that bottle of alcohol,' the doctor said calmly. 'I've got to clean this wound. That's a nasty blow you took on your shoulder. If you weren't built like a horse it would have snapped your collarbone ... Thanks, Captain. This is going to burn, Dan.'

The alcohol did burn, and Dan winced under it. He saw Red Halsey and felt the soothing warmth of water sponging off the mud. The doctor muttered, 'Superficial. I'll not need to sew it,' and bandage tightened around Dan's arm. He felt knowing fingers work on his shoulders, and Ruffin's concerned face was always in sight. Then Ruffin stepped aside and Nevada, wide-eyed and pale, was there.

'Dan! You're hurt, Dan!'

'I'll be O.K., Nevada,' Dan comforted. 'I'm not hurt bad.'

Behind Nevada he could see Penny's drawn face. He managed a smile for Penny, although the fingers that manipulated his shoulder hurt like the mischief.

'Not broken,' the doctor said with

satisfaction. 'I thought not. Now, ladies, if you'll get out of here, we'll put him to bed. You can see him. Sure, you can see him in the morning. He's all right, Nevada; just jolted pretty badly ... Yes, I said he was all right. Now let us get him to bed.'

'Put him in my bed, Doc,' Ruffin ordered. 'How do you feel, Dan?'

'Kind of ... drunk!' Dan answered.

'I gave you enough to make anybody drunk.' Ruffin's voice was gruff. 'All right, Doc. The girls are gone. Let's get his clothes off.'

'I can undress myself,' Dan said indignantly, feeling hands pulling at his trousers.

The doctor laughed. 'That must have been a big drink,' he said. 'Now, up you come! Help me here, Red.'

Dan felt himself lifted and carried. Then cool sheets engulfed him and he looked up at Ruffin and Red.

'Said he walked because there wasn't room in the hacks. I found him about a quarter this side of the lot.' Dan heard Ruffin's voice as from a distance.

The big drink and the opiate took hold, and Dan drifted pleasantly away, listening to the rumbling voices.

When he wakened every bone and muscle complained and ached. He turned in the bed and sat up. Almost immediately the doctor and then Tom Ruffin joined him, and the doctor, having felt his pulse and touched his forehead, grinned. 'How do you feel?' he asked.

'Like hell,' Dan answered honestly.

'You're all right,' the physician chuckled. 'You feel as bad from that drink Tom gave you as you do from the beating you got. He handed you a water glass of whisky and you drank it all.'

'Can I get up?' Dan asked. 'I feel all right. Just stiff, that's all.'

'I don't think so,' the doctor told him. 'You won't want to move around much.'

'I want to get up and put on my clothes,' Dan said obstinately.

It was so arranged. Red Halsey came down from the bachelor car, bringing Dan's clothes and many questions. Dan dressed, finding that he could not use his left arm, and was forced to call upon Red to help. He felt better when he had eaten breakfast and was quite able to cope with Ruffin and Purrington when they came. He told his story deliberately and, when he had finished, made a comment.

'One of 'em yelled "Slough him" just as they jumped me. I think they were from the lot, Tom.'

'That's what Cap an' I think,' Ruffin agreed gravely. 'Have you had any trouble with any of the roustabouts?'

'No. But I got paid yesterday. I had my bank roll in my pocket, and maybe somebody saw it.'

158

'Do you want to go to the police?' Ruffin asked. 'I don't want to call 'em unless you say so. A thing like this gives the show a black eye an'...'

'I don't want to call the police,' Dan interrupted. 'All I want to do is look the bunch over. I marked one of them, and I'll know him if I see him.'

Ruffin and Purrington exchanged glances. 'I think you can do that,' Ruffin announced, relief apparent in his voice.

'At noon,' Purrington said, 'they'll all be in the cookhouse. Think you can travel to the lot, Dan?'

Dan glanced at the window still wet with rivulets of falling rain. 'I don't want to walk,' he grinned, 'but I can get out to the lot all right.'

'Then we'll go,' Ruffin decided. 'Can you fix him up, Doc?'

The physician grumbled something about a young fool that ought to stay in bed but moved efficiently to help. Dan, his arm in a sling, his muscles complaining as he moved, put on a coat and waited. Red had gone to get a hack. When Red returned he looked anxiously at Dan.

'Think you can make it?'

'I'll make it,' Dan promised, 'but I feel like I'd been throwed an' stepped on. Easy, Red! Don't grab that arm.'

The five men crowded the hack. Red and

159

Purrington rode beside Dan, while the portly doctor and Ruffin occupied the front seat.

There were but few people in the short side of the cookhouse when Dan and his party entered. Most of the performers had chosen to remain at the train rather than come to the lot through the rain. Smokey Darnell was there with Belle, together with Bob White, Shorty, and half a dozen more. Dan, with Ruffin beside him, strolled into the long side which was crowded as usual, while Purrington, the doctor, and Red Halsey remained at the entrance. The boss canvasman and Brannigan, leaving their table, joined their boss.

'Somethin', Mr. Ruffin?' Brannigan asked.

Dan scanned the faces turned toward him as he entered. He saw one and then another, puffed and discolored from blows. Not one of the other men was marked by fresh bruises, although there were old marks on several. 'Those two,' Dan said to Ruffin. 'The big man and that other. See them, Tom?'

'I see them,' Ruffin growled, and then, to Brannigan and the boss canvasman: 'Come outside a minute.' He tilted his head back toward the entrance.

'Last night,' Ruffin said when they were outside, 'Dan here was jumped by a couple of men while he went to town. They tried to kill him. One of them had a knife and the other a billy or a club. He got clear of them and he marked them up. There's two men in there that

160

have been beat up plenty.'

'That's Bugs an' Fatso,' the boss canvasman said. 'They had a fight. Bugs has been ridin' Fatso, an' I guess Fatso had enough. Anyhow, he worked Bugs over.'

'It couldn't have been the little man,' Purrington said quietly. 'Could it, Tom?'

Ruffin looked at the captain and seemed to recall something, for his eyes widened. 'No,' he said hastily. 'It couldn't have been Fatso.'

'Why not?' Dan rasped. 'They're all that's marked.'

'Didn't you hear what Joe said?' Ruffin rasped. 'Those two had a fight yesterday. That's how they got banged up.' Placing a hand on Dan's good arm, he propelled him away. 'We were wrong,' Ruffin continued. 'It wasn't anybody on the lot. Just a couple of tramps, likely.'

Reluctantly Dan allowed himself to be drawn into the short side of the cookhouse.

The rain stopped before the afternoon performance. Dan, refusing to return to the train, stayed at the lot, loafing in the pad room for the most part. Nevada came to reason with him, but Dan would not go back to the train even for her. Realizing the uselessness of argument, she suggested that they view the performance from the stands, and accordingly the two sat in the big top and watched their fellows go through their paces for the benefit of a lot of small boys. There was scarcely an adult in the crowd.

'Kids,' Nevada said. 'If it weren't for the kids, the show couldn't run. I like kids, Dan.'

She sat close to Dan, her hand tucked confidingly under his good arm, and, instead of watching the performers, looked at the man beside her. Dan was uncomfortable under that scrutiny. Nevada laughed. 'I'll go away and leave you alone if I embarrass you,' she offered.

'No,' Dan said. 'I don't want you to go away, Nevada.'

After the show they found the wind cold and blustery. Clouds hung low against the northern horizon and scudded past overhead. As evening came the whole world seemed to take on a coppery glow. There was much activity on the lot. Men, their hats pulled down against the force of the wind, swung mauls, driving tent stakes. Guy ropes were tightened again. The boss canvasman, hands on hips, surveyed the big top, and Ruffin joined him. There seemed to be a disagreement between Ruffin and the canvasman, and presently, fighting the force of the wind, Ruffin came to the pad tent where Dan sat with Nevada.

'Joe wanted to tear down,' he said. 'He's afraid of a cyclone. This ain't cyclone country. I told him we'd leave her stand.'

'I've been trying to get Dan to go home,' Nevada said. 'Won't you help me, Tom?'

'You ought to go back to the train, Dan,'

162

Ruffin agreed with Nevada. 'You've been out all day, an' Doc said for you to stay quiet.'

'I'll go back after a while,' Dan answered. 'I feel all right.'

His body was stiff and sore, but Dan did not want to go back to the train. He watched the canvasmen as they moved about, scanning them for signs of bruises or of stiffness. He was far from satisfied with what had been done at noon. Dan had heard the words screamed in the darkness: 'Slough him! Tear him down!' That was show talk. And he had seen the puffed and bruised faces of Bugs and Fatso. Why were Ruffin and Purrington so sure that Fatso had not been one of his attackers? Fatso and Bugs were right for size; one was big and one was smaller. Dan, absorbed with his thoughts, paid no heed to Nevada.

'You aren't listening to a word I say,' she accused. 'I'm going to leave you alone. I want to take care of you and you won't let me. You act as though you didn't care what I wanted, Dan!'

Dan looked up. 'Sure I do,' he answered, 'but I want to stay here, Nevada. I just want to sit here.'

'Well, sit there, then!' Nevada snapped, and started away. Instantly she returned. 'I'm sorry, Dan,' she apologized. 'I seem to do the wrong thing all the time. You stay here and I'll come for you when supper's ready.' She flashed a smile and left.

The coppery sun went down, and with it the wind died and a flat calm prevailed. Twilight held briefly, and night came like the descent of a curtain. The lights of the show glittered, and as the time for the performance drew near, buggies, wagons, and people on foot began to stream slowly toward the show ground. Rain had held the crowd away, but now the rain was over, and men and women, urged by small boys and girls and by their own half-concealed desires, came to the lot, braving the muddy streets and roads. The stand was in a cotton country, and share-croppers and owners, men, women, and children, came to see Ruffin's Wild West and, for a while, get away from mule and Georgia stock, hoe and toil. Christmas, Fourth of July, and the Circus; these were their only holidays, and they would not be cheated of one of them.

Outside the big top the barkers had begun their pitch. People streamed slowly past the gatemen. Nevada and Dan, sitting in the blues well toward the top of the stand, watched the crowd come in. The program venders were working, and already the concession men were hawking their wares.

'I haven't,' Nevada said to Dan, 'seen a show from the seats since I was a little girl. Not until today. It would be fun if you weren't hurt.'

Dan smiled down at her. 'I'm not hurt much,' he said. 'When we quit the show business an' have our own place we'll take in every show an' carny that comes to our country, won't we?'

'When we quit the show business?' Nevada said.

'Sure.'

The girl was thoughtful for a moment and then looked up again. This was the first time Dan had ever spoken to her of the future.

'Dan,' Nevada said, 'when will we ...?' She got no farther. At the end of the tent the band blared, and Tom Ruffin, hat lifted, led his performers in.

Nevada and Dan watched the show. They saw the bucking, the roping, the Roman riding, the Cossacks, the Indians. They watched Smokey Darnell and Belle work their act. They saw Ruth Shattuck and Penny and their opponents fly around the track in the relay. Above them the canvas bellied gently and slapped down as the wind increased.

The stage holdup came on and was carried to its conclusion. The wind grew stronger. A woman shepherded her brood down from the seats, glancing fearfully at the canvas.

'I don't like this,' Nevada whispered. 'Let's get out of here, Dan.'

'We're all right,' Dan reassured from the depth of his ignorance.

Other customers, apprehensive, were leaving the tent. Tom Ruffin halted his big horse in the center of the arena and stopped the show to make an announcement.

'There is no cause for alarm, ladies and gentlemen,' Ruffin bellowed through his megaphone. 'None at all. This tent is securely fastened. You're as safe here as you would be in your own homes. And now I take pleasure in presenting Captain Jack Purrington, the most famous shot in the world today: big-game hunter, explorer, pistol and rifle shot. Captain Jack Purrington!'

The band struck up once more, and Penny, mounted on a black horse and dressed in white buckskin, entered the arena, the captain behind her.

They rode slowly around the arena, Penny tossing blocks of wood into the air, the captain shooting at them with a rifle. Dan and Penny knew that the charges were light and that the bullets the captain used were made of tallow and lead shot. They knew, too, that he could hit those blocks with solid lead and full-power charges and that his trick loads were a concession to the canvas over the arena rather than to any lack of skill.

The canvas was slatting now, slapping up and down violently, and, regardless of Ruffin's announcement, people were leaving the seats and crowding down into the space between seats and track. Purrington dismounted, as did Penny. The girl placed a sheet of tin against a backstop. Ruffin was bellowing through his megaphone, unable to make himself heard over the noise of wind and crowd. A sudden

166

lull came in the fury of the wind, as does the roar of flame in a stovepipe when the damper is closed. The lights flickered, and then with a crash wind and rain struck. The poles at either end and in the center of the tent swayed, and above the screaming voices came a sharp cracking noise. Dan stood up, pulling Nevada to her feet.

Tom Ruffin, arena attendants, performers who had run in from the entry—all were trying to quiet the crowd that fought toward the exists, were trying desperately to avert panic.

'Drop down behind the seats,' Dan rasped in Nevada's ear. 'Duck under the side an' get clear. She's goin'.' He released the girl and, bending, heaved up a blue painted plank and let it rattle down across the seats. Nevada, brave despite the danger, lowered herself into the opening thus made and dropped to the ground. 'Come on, Dan,' she called. 'Come on!'

For just an instant Dan hesitated. In that instant the pole at the back end of the tent buckled and collapsed. Lights went out, and the crowd stampeded in pure panic. Nevada had a glimpse of Dan's face as he looked down at her. She called again, frantically:

'Dan! Dan!'

Dan's lips formed a single word, inaudible in the confusion, and his arm pointed toward the arena. Nevada read that word and gesture. Dan had shouted 'Penny!' Nevada saw him turn and run down across the seats, and then a guy rope broke and the great center pole swayed and came crashing down, bringing the tent with it.

CHAPTER TWELVE

The lights were extinguished as the tent went down, and in the utter darkness Nevada screamed, calling to Dan, frightened more for the man than for herself. When he did not answer, the girl struggled with the heavy canvas of the side, lifted it, and crawled out into the rain. Lights bobbed and hoarse voices shouted. She heard a man yell: 'Blow-down!' and as she turned to face him: 'Did the crowd git out?'

'Dan's in there!' Nevada screamed. 'Dan Mar!'

The shouter lifted his lantern high to look at her. 'There's a lot of people in there, lady,' he said almost gently, and then, with a savagery that belied his voice, pushed her aside and ran on. The front of the tent still stood, canted at a crazy angle, weaving back and forth in the blasts of wind like a drunken man in a narrow hall. Nevada ran toward the lights that still burned in front of the tent. As she ran she saw Tom Ruffin facing the entrance and behind Ruffin a myriad of white faces blurred by rain.

Nevada reached Ruffin and caught at his sleeve.

'Tom! Dan's in there, Tom!'

Ruffin paid no attention. 'It hit so quick!' he said, his voice strained and hoarse. 'Who'd of thought it would hit so quick?'

'Dan's in there!' Nevada screamed, trying to make Ruffin understand. 'Help him, Tom. He ...' She stopped, for Dan Mar, carrying Penny, a dead weight in his arms, came out of the tilted entrance and walked like a blind man toward the crowd. He had scarcely cleared the tent before the entrance collapsed. Nevada ran toward him and a man from the crowd also ran forward. Nevada heard the newcomer's words.

'I'm a doctor. Is she hurt? Here, man, let me see!'

Dan would not release Penny. He held her high against his chest, his injured arm supporting the girl, and Nevada, seeing his face, turned swiftly away.

Ruffin, recovered from his momentary shock, was bellowing orders, and the assembled roustabouts went into action like a trained army. They knew what to do and how to do it. Everyone worked, performers, roustabouts, all, hampered by the rain, the wind, and the townspeople who crowded in, some hysterically calling for missing members of their family.

Most of the crowd was out. A few had been caught under the canvas, but the seats had not

169

fallen when the tent came down, and these and their supports had served as a shelter. The greater number of those injured had been hurt in the rush for the exits, but even among these there were no very serious injuries. Nevada, following Ruffin's orders, went to the cookhouse where the show physician and the doctor from town had set up a dressing station. There she found Penny Thwaite sitting up, a bandage around her head and her eyes still holding a dazed expression. Dan was not there, and Nevada went to work with the rest of the women.

When Dan returned he went directly to Penny, knelt beside her, and spoke. Penny answered, and the man, apparently reassured, went out again. Ruffin was talking to the town's police chief and to his own attorney, the fixer whom he carried with the show. The canvas boss entered, water streaming from his slicker and hat.

'It ain't so bad,' he announced. 'Everybody got out. How many was hurt, Doc?'

'Not many,' the show physician answered. 'Not badly, either. I had one boy with a broken arm. The rest were bruises and contusions. How did you find it, Doctor?' turning to his confrere.

The townsman shrugged. 'No one badly hurt,' he said. 'That girl was the worst.' He gestured toward Penny. 'She was hit on the head and I think has a concussion. You'll have

170

to watch her.'

Nevada ceased to listen, for Dan had come into the cook-house again and, pausing, looked at her searchingly. 'You're all right, Nevada?'

'I'm all right, Dan.'

Dan let go a long breath. 'I'm sure glad,' he said.

'Coffee, Dan?' Nevada turned from the man. She knew, without any telling, that Dan Mar had only just recalled her. 'Here.' She thrust out a steaming cup.

'Thanks,' he said dumbly.

'That's O.K.' Nevada's eyes sharpened. 'You'd better have Doc look at that arm. It's bleeding again.'

In the morning the sun was out, bright and big and benign. In the daylight the show people took account of the damage that had been done. The big top was down, flat on the muddy lot, and the property top and the dressing rooms were damaged. Beyond the lot the damage was worse. A minor tornado had struck the little town, marching across it in a narrow strip. Ruffin had been right when he shouted that the people in the tent were safer than they would be in their own homes. Three houses had been destroyed, trees broken and flattened, and the roof of a tobacco shed lifted and carried completely away. The vagaries of the storm had caused it to strike between the big top and the stock tent and not with full fury. Apparently the whirling wind had lifted and dipped again. Show and town had almost been spared.

The canvasmen worked, spreading the big top to dry and taking account of damage. There were some rents in the canvas, one great gash where the center pole had pierced, and a panel required replacement; but, taken as a whole, the material damage was slight.

This did not hold true for other damage. Claims poured in on Tom Ruffin. It seemed as though a lawyer had contacted every parent who had a boy with a stubbed toe, and every stubbed toe was blamed on the blowdown. Ruffin and his lawyer were busy while the canvasmen worked. Legitimate claims were investigated and promptly settled, but those which seemed invalid were set aside.

Ruffin knew from past experience that a show was considered fair game by every shyster, and he knew, too, that local juries had a habit of giving verdicts in favor of their townspeople. But Ruffins could be just as hard and tough as the next one. His words to the men who presented unjust claims were: 'Go ahead and sue. It'll cost you money and I'll fight.'

The performers had a well-earned rest. They had worked with the rest during the emergency; now they stepped back to let the regular crews handle matters. Many of the troupe, the women in particular, had costumes ruined by the storm. Mud and rain had wrought havoc, and among the show people there was no rejoicing at the enforced vacation.

Nevada had little to say during the wait, but she watched Dan covertly, question in her eyes. Dan, for his part, was worried about Penny, who convalesced in her car under the attention of the show doctor. That worthy assured Dan that the girl's condition was not serious and scolded the man for breaking open the wound in his arm.

'Go and see her,' the doctor commanded on the occasion of Dan's fourth visit to inquire about Penny's welfare. 'She's all right. And keep that arm in a sling if you want to be able to use it any time soon.'

Dan found Penny and Ruth in their compartment. Ruth, brisk as usual, answered the door.

'Doc said I could come an' see how Penny is makin' it,' Dan announced. 'How is she, Ruth?'

'She's all right. Shaken up some, but she's all right. Doc said to keep her quiet.'

'I'll not stay long,' Dan assured. 'How are you feelin', Penny?'

Penny smiled at him. 'I'm fine,' she said. 'How are you, Dan? Is your arm any better?'

'The arm's all right.' Dan sat gingerly on the edge of the bed. 'My shoulder's still sore.'

'If you're going to stay a minute I'll go find Mrs. Flarity,' Ruth announced. 'I want to get some thread.' She did not wait for an answer but left the compartment. When Ruth was gone there came a strained silence.

'You had me worried,' Dan said awkwardly. 'Nevada an' I were watching the show when the wind hit. I was scared, Penny.'

'Ruth told me that you brought me out.' Penny smiled at the man. 'Thanks, Dan. I guess I was unconscious. The last thing I can remember is the crowd coming into the arena and the tent falling.'

'You were up against the seats on the far side.' Dan's voice was matter-of-fact. 'I found you right by the barrier.'

Silence again. 'I pretty near went out of my head,' Dan said. 'I thought you were dead. I guess I ... Penny, look here a minute.'

Penny kept her eyelids lowered; her fingers toyed with a tuft on the quilt.

'Penny!' Dan commanded.

The girl would not look up. 'How is Nevada, Dan?' she asked, her voice unnaturally strained.

'Nevada's all right. We aren't talkin' about Nevada.'

'I think we'd better.' Penny played with the little cotton tuft. 'When are you and Nevada going to be married?'

Dan, who had been leaning toward the girl, straightened suddenly. 'Nevada an' me?'

Penny risked a swift glance. 'I know you've been keeping it a secret,' she said quickly. 'I

174

haven't told anyone. I ... I happened to be outside the car that night and ... Well, I saw you and Nevada. I hope you'll be very happy.'

'You saw us?'

'Yes.'

Ruth appeared at the door. 'That Irish mick!' she snapped wrathfully as she flounced into the compartment. 'You'd think she ran the show! All I wanted was a spool of number sixty, white. It's a fine thing when you have to fight to get a spool of thread.'

Dan got up as Ruth seated herself. 'I guess I'll go,' he announced slowly. 'I'm glad that you're feelin' better, Penny.'

'I feel fine.' Penny smiled up at him. 'I'll be out tomorrow. Tell Nevada hello for me.'

Dan went out. Ruth, glancing down at her friend, saw Penny's eyes follow the man. 'It's funny,' Ruth snapped, 'that Nevada hasn't come to see you. Everybody else has been here.'

*   *   *

Canvas dry and repaired, claims settled, all in order once more, the show moved on. Due to the blowdown Ruffin had canceled two dates, and the first jump was a long one. In his car Ruffin scowled as he cast up the damage. Kerr, the book-keeper, sitting beside Ruffin's desk, also frowned as he made calculations. The blowdown had cost a lot of money, too much

175

money. Besides the damage done there was the loss from the two canceled dates.

'Well, Tom?' Kerr said.

'I'll fix it,' Ruffin growled.

Kerr went out, and Ruffin stared at the desk top, his forehead creased in thought. Presently he produced a letterhead from a drawer and his pen scratched busily. While he was so engaged the forward door opened and Nevada came in. Glancing up at his visitor, Ruffin's frown changed to a smile.

'Busy, Tom?' Nevada asked.

'Not too busy to talk to you. Sit down. What's on your mind?'

The girl seated herself. 'The blowdown hit you pretty hard, didn't it?' she asked.

'Not too hard.' Ruffin's voice was cheerful. 'I'm all right.'

Nevada moved her boot toe in a little circle on the car floor, watching it carefully. 'I wanted to tell you,' she said, 'that I've got a little money. If you need it you're welcome. And if it's any help, you can hold up my pay for a while.'

'Well, thanks, Nevada!' Ruffin said, surprised. 'That won't be necessary. It's swell of you to offer.'

Nevada continued to move her boot in its small circle. 'I'm kind of bothered, Tom,' she announced. 'I ... Tom, what do you do when there's something that you want? Take it?'

'I always try to.' Ruffin, too, watched the

176

moving boot. 'I found out a long time ago that nobody would look after me if I didn't look out for myself.'

'That's what I've always done.' Nevada's dark, long-lashed eyes searched Ruffin's face. 'Maybe I've been a heel for doing it.'

'You couldn't be a heel if you tried.'

'No?' The long lashes lowered. 'I don't know. Have you seen Dan lately?'

'Why, yes. Of course I've seen him.'

'Talk to him?'

'No. What would I talk to him about?'

'I don't know'—vaguely. 'I just thought maybe he'd talked to you. I'll go along now. You're busy and I oughtn't to bother you.'

'You're never a bother, Nevada,' Ruffin said, rising. 'When are you and Dan going to hitch up?'

'I don't know,' Nevada said. 'I thought ... Oh, I don't know, Tom.' She left the car, and Ruffin stared after her, wondering why she had visited him. Then, engrossed with his own problem, he returned to his letter writing.

* * *

The red cars with the yellow letters on their sides slid through the pleasant countryside. In the last car Ruffin destroyed what he had written and started over. Penny and Ruth sat in their compartment, Ruth sewing and fussing because Mary Flarity was so hard-boiled, and

177

Penny staring absently out the window. Nevada, in her compartment, also watched with unseeing eyes the landscape flashing past; and in the room next to her the two Darnells quarreled, their haranguing muffled by the noises of the train. In the laborers' bunk cars Emil Garza sprawled on his bunk and scanned the ceiling as he considered the progress on his case; and in the car ahead of Garza, Bugs Nixon, his bruises turned to old yellow and blue, growled from the side of his mouth to his partner, Tony Hart.

Back in the bachelor car Dan Mar loafed on a seat and listened to the mild joshing of the pitch players, his mind traveling from thought to thought as the car wheels clicked over the rail joints. Tangibles and intangibles, Dan considered both. He thought of Penny and how sweet she was, how loyal and square. He remembered how he had held her, feather-light, against his chest, and how her eyelashes had curved against her cheek. She was a child to be protected and watched over, and she was a woman too, beautiful and desirable.

He thought of Nevada, her strength and her talent and the hardness that covered sensitiveness. Nevada was fine. She was like a man, long known, many times tested. And how could a man hurt a girl like that? It was impossible. For a while, then, Dan Mar despised himself.

The pitch game broke up, and Red Halsey

came back and sat down beside Dan. 'How you makin' it?' he asked. 'Goin' to go to work tomorrow?'

'I don't know.' Dan touched his injured shoulder. 'I'm still pretty stiff.'

'You know,' Red drawled, 'what with the blowdown an' all the excitement, I pretty near forgot what happened to you.'

'So did I.' Dan grinned.

Red's eyes were keen. 'It was kind of funny,' he drawled. 'The way Ruffin an' Cap acted, I mean. Them two boys in the cookhouse was marked up plenty. Kind of funny that they'd just had a fight, wasn't it?'

Dan nodded.

'*An*',' Red said pointedly, 'kind of lucky too. Ever think of that?'

'I've thought about it.'

'You know,' Red drawled, 'Ruffin asked if you'd had any trouble around the lot an' you said you hadn't. You'd forgot Smokey, hadn't you?'

Slowly Dan's eyes narrowed. 'I forgot him,' he agreed. 'But Smokey was at the cookhouse when I was jumped.'

'That's right, he was.' Red busied himself with tobacco and paper. 'I've noticed somethin', though. Smokey's pretty friendly with a lot of them roustabouts.'

'So?' Dan said.

Red lit his cigarette. 'You choked Smokey one time.' He inhaled and let the smoke fog in a

179

thin vapor from his lips. 'Smokey's the kind to get even, Dan.'

Dan shrugged and was instantly sorry because of the stiff shoulder. 'Smokey has been carryin' a gun for me,' he drawled. 'I've seen it under his shirt. I haven't forgotten Smokey. I've watched him.'

'Well'—Red grinned—'I thought I'd mention it.'

'Hey, Red,' Bob White called from the front of the car, 'are you goin' to play?'

Red got up. 'I'm two bits winner,' he said. 'Well, Dan, any time you need some help ...' He grinned at his friend and went up the aisle, swaying with the motion of the train.

There, Dan thought, was a real one! He was tempted to talk to Red, tell him what he knew, and ask advice. But Red, for all his good qualities, talked a lot and had all the finesse of a bull calf in a flower bed. It was not time to take Red into his confidence. And, besides, just what did Dan know for a certainty?

Briefly he reviewed the facts. The masks used at Brule had come from Ruffin's show. Item one. That fact was in Art Murrah's hands. It was odd that Murrah had not answered Dan's letter. Item two: A set of spur tracks across a saddle seat, tracks not made by the man who rode the saddle. Item three: An attack by two men who, from their language, followed the show. Item four: Two men marked by battle, and the queer insistence of Tom Ruffin and

Captain Purrington that these were not the men who had attacked Dan Mar.

Nothing fitted into place. Perhaps there was no connection between any two of them. Perhaps they all belonged to different puzzles. But sitting there, leaning back in the seat while the car rolled smoothly along, Dan Mar could not help but feel that somehow the facts interlocked, that somewhere there was a key and that he held it. He scowled. A man who had a key and didn't know where it fitted was as ignorant as a man who had no key at all.

CHAPTER THIRTEEN

Missouri has some good towns, and Willow Bluffs is as good as any of them. Ruffin's Wild West, unloading at that county seat and division point, pitched on the show grounds and prepared to give Willow Bluffs a sight of the real Old West. On the morning of arrival in Willow Bluffs, Dan tried his shoulder and found that it worked, although twinges of pain shot through it as he spun his rope. Pleased with his discovery, he found Nevada and asked her to rehearse with him.

Nevada was solicitous. Was Dan sure that he was ready? Did his shoulder pain? Hadn't they better wait a few days more? Dan reassured his partner, and before noon they went through the act.

At noon Ruffin's Wild West paraded. People filled the square where the tall willows that gave the town its name surrounded the courthouse. Wagons, buggies, saddle horses, every kind of vehicle and equipment, lined the hitch rails. Small boys, barefooted, dodged in and out, and little girls in calico or stiffly-starched gingham clutched ten-cent pieces in small hands and waited, big-eyed. Men and women, in from the country or come downtown to see the parade, stood in groups or moved in and out of the stores. A good town, Willow Bluffs, and, to Tom Ruffin's performers, a lot like coming home. They were on the last leg of the circuit now, turning north, heading back to their own country. The feel of it was in the air and in the tanned, wind-wrinkled, up-turned faces of the people. At noon Tom Ruffin, on his big white horse, led the parade into the square.

Ruffin's Wild West knew how to parade. Behind Tom came the Sioux, gaudy in paint and feathers and buckskin, mounted on pintos and roans and any and all kinds of odd-colored horses. Trust an Indian to have a showy pony! The band followed the Indians, and after the band came the stage, drawn by three spans of shining black mules. Then came the performers, all mounted, all dressed in their very best. Horses, sleek with grooming and good feed, curveted and pranced; show horses,

182

showing off. Bit and spur chains jingled; well-polished saddles, bridles, martingales, caught sunlight on silver or nickel mountings. Wide hats, white or black or brown, shielded smiling faces from the good Missouri sun. Silk shirts vaunted their many colors, and chaps flapped as the horses swung out of the line and were reined back. At the end of the parade came the covered wagon, drawn by two yoke of oxen and housing a calliope that shrilled music when the band stopped playing. Up one street and down another the parade passed, around the square, circling the old brownstone courthouse, past the stores and business houses, the bank and the post office, a fixed smile on every face, every back straight, every boot deep in a stirrup.

'A good town, Dan,' Nevada said from the corner of her mouth, lips scarcely moving. 'We'll have a crowd.'

'A good town,' Dan answered absently.

At the bank corner Nigger swung out of line and Dan reined him back. The shades of the bank were drawn, for it was closed for noon; and in front of it Dan saw the familiar figure of a pudgy, roughly dressed man: Fatso, the roustabout from the show. Fatso Garza was expressionlessly watching the parade. Nigger, in line now, passed the corner, and Dan looked down the crowded street. There was the side door of the bank, and beyond that door stood a little group of roustabouts. Among these was

Bugs, the fat man. Something clicked in Dan's mind. Here in Willow Bluffs was a setup comparable to Brule, a bank that closed at noon, a corner building with a side door. And here by the bank were two men already under Dan's suspicion. Dan turned to look back and rode twisted in the saddle for so long that Nevada spoke.

'Straighten up, Dan. What's the idea?'

* * *

The big top was packed that afternoon and again that night. The white wagon was swamped, and venders did an amazing business and hardly had to hawk their wares.

'Give me a mule country every time,' Red Halsey said to Dan as they met in the entrance. 'These are the kind of folks for my money.'

'You bet,' Dan replied. The Cowboy and the Lady had been greeted with shouts, and Dan and Nevada had taken four bows. Dan was feeling good.

That night it was hard to go to bed and the cars were lighted for a long time. Ruffin's Wild West, having met with disaster, was back and going again, in the money, rolling. Everybody felt it.

The feeling persisted. In the morning, in place of the customary short before-breakfast greetings, the performers were jovial and bandied jests back and forth.

'By golly!' Red announced as he an and Dan strolled from the cookhouse, 'I feel I just like I used to when we'd finished the fall work an' were paid off. We sure come out of the sag, Dan.'

'We sure did,' Dan Mar agreed.

'What are you goin' to do this mornin'?' Red asked. 'Let's go uptown, huh?'

Dan shook his head. 'I think I'll stick around the lot,' he answered. 'I've got some things to do.'

'I'm goin' to town,' Red stated. 'There's a mule sale comin' off. I think I'll see it. Better come, Dan.'

'No,' Dan answered, still looking toward the pad room. 'You go on, Red. I'll stick around the lot.'

'See you later then,' Red announced and, spying Bob White emerging from the cookhouse, hailed him. 'Hey, Bob! Wait a minute an' I'll ride with you.' Red hurried away, and Dan strolled toward the pad room.

The pad room was empty. Dan sat down on his chest and looked out beneath the rolled canvas. Purrington and Ruffin strolled by, deep in conversation. Ruth Shattuck, Penny, Belle Darnell, and two more women made a talkative group walking past. Smokey Darnell, all alone, hurried past the pad room. Then came a lull. Dan had not seen the men he wanted to see. Leaving the pad room, he walked to the stock tent and looked in.

Hostlers were busy in the stock tent, and, having paid a brief visit to Domino and Nigger, Dan went out. He found a quiet spot where the sun was hot and, squatting on his boot heels, let the warmth engulf him, quiet as any Indian loafing. The morning droned along. Almost everyone had gone downtown, and the lot was deserted. Fatso went into the pad room and did not come out, and presently Dan got up and followed.

The roustabout was sitting on a box beside a chest, writing on a tablet. Dan walked idly along. As he approached, Fatso looked up and then, seemingly casual, covered the tablet with his hand.

'Writin' home?' Dan drawled, stopping.

'Just writin'.'

Dan walked on, leaving the pad room at its farther end. Fatso frowned and returned to his writing.

... Although there has been no activity since I joined the show, I am quite positive that our men are still here. No one has been discharged or quit. Since I have established the-fact that the mask found at the scene of the murder is identical with those used in the act, I have made very little progress. I strongly urge that at least two more operatives be sent to work with me. It is impossible for me to shadow every suspect, and I have been devoting most of my attention to Mar, the man mentioned in

my former reports. I believe that Mar suspects he is being watched. As mentioned in my last report, he was injured in an attempted robbery. Either he was actually attacked or was hurt during a fight with his confederates. Unfortunately I had been forced to fight with the man Bugs Nixon, also under suspicion, and as I had marked him considerably, I was unable to tell whether or not he was one of the men attacking Mar.

Fatso chewed his pencil, scowled at what he had written, and added a final line.

I trust that the operatives I have asked for will be assigned immediately.
Respectfully,
EMIL GARZA

The letter finished, Garza addressed an envelope, sealed and stamped it, and, leaving the pad room, walked briskly toward the square. It would not do for a letter addressed to the Pinkerton Agency to fall into other hands than those for which it was intended, nor would it do for anyone to see that address and become curious. He did not look back, but had he done so he might have seen Dan Mar loitering along behind him.

Dan was curious. He wondered why Fatso had covered that letter, to whom Fatso was writing, and why. He remembered, too, that he had seen both Fatso and Bugs at the Willow Bluffs Bank. It was almost noon.

Garza hurried along. He turned the corner of the square and, glancing back, saw Dan standing on the corner south of the bank and a full block away from it. A thought flashed into Garza's mind. During the parade he had seen Dan turn in his saddle and look at the bank. Why had Mar done that? And why had Mar followed him from the lot? Garza hurried across the intersection to the post office which faced the courthouse, two doors east of the corner. As he entered the post office he bumped into Captain Purrington.

Purrington, knocked back a step, grunted and caught Garza to recover his balance. 'Watch where you're going!' the captain began angrily and then, recognizing the man he had seized, released his hold. 'What's all the hurry?' he demanded.

Garza took two steps and dropped the letter in a slot. 'Something up,' he snapped. 'Come on!'

For an instant Purrington hesitated, then followed the detective out of the post office. As they cleared the door shots sounded, and both men ran toward the corner. Just as they reached it a bunch of mules, being driven south, struck the intersection. With an oath Garza plunged into the street ahead of the mules and dodged around them. Purrington, following Garza, was too late. The mules filled the northwestern intersection and blocked his passage.

Purrington ran across the street to the south and, reaching the fence that surrounded the courthouse grounds, scrambled up into the bed of a wagon. The horses hitched to the wagon, frightened by the shots and Purrington's sudden appearance, fought to break their tie rope, and the wagon lurched and jerked. Purrington braced widespread legs and faced the bank. He saw men come from the bank and Garza run toward them. One man wheeled and, facing Garza, fired a shot.

Purrington had a glimpse of a masked face and saw Garza fall. The captain's own gun slid out into his hand and fell level. He fired once and then again, quickly. The man who had shot Garza went down, and as Purrington fired for a third time another of the bandits staggered and fell. The third man was still running west along the street.

Purrington sighted again, and as his finger contracted on the trigger the wagon team, breaking free, stampeded, running straight east along the side of the square. Purrington's feet were jerked from under him and he struck the wagon box with a thud, while his shot went harmlessly into the air. Scrambling up, the captain possessed himself of the lines, pulled the team to the right into the wagons parked along the north side of the square, and, jumping from the box, ran back toward the intersection.

A block south of the bank Dan Mar heard the first shots. He ran across the street, struck the board sidewalk, and pounded along. As he ran he met obstacles. Men and women and frightened children were trying to get away from the shooting. Dan bumped into them and, seeking clearer passage, tried the street. The street was full of mules, and he was forced to stay on the sidewalk. Before he reached the bank corner Garza was down and Purrington was shooting from the wagon bed. Dan reached the corner just as the team stampeded, throwing the captain. Dan saw the third bandit from the bank running west and started to follow, but a frightened townsman, blundering into Dan, knocked him sprawling to the sidewalk.

As Dan scrambled up he saw Garza in the street. The mules were milling in the intersection, threatening momentarily to trample the injured man, and Dan, plunging in without regard for consequences, caught hold of Garza and dragged him to the sidewalk, clear of plunging mules and flashing hoofs. As he let Garza down he felt himself seized and, turning, saw Nevada's frightened face. Dan straightened, and Nevada's arms went around his neck. She was frightened, and there was nothing for Dan to do but comfort her. He half carried, half led her into the doorway of the store next to the bank. While he quieted the girl a crowd formed in the street, and when presently Nevada was calmed Dan looked toward the corner and saw only men surrounding the scene of the tragedy.

'That fellow was from the show,' Dan said. 'He's hurt. I ought to ...' He took a step to leave, and Nevada caught his arm.

'Please, Dan. Please don't go. Take me back to the lot. There's plenty of people to look after that man.'

Dan glanced at the crowd on the corner, saw Purrington forcing his way through, and turned back to the girl.

'Sure, I'll take you,' he agreed. 'Come on. We'll go back to the lot.'

When Purrington reached the corner he found Garza on the sidewalk where Dan had left him. Pushing his way through the crowd, the captain kneeled beside the man and opened his shirt. A glance showed that the detective was hard hit. Blood welled from a wound in his chest, and his half-opened eyes were glazed.

'Where's a doctor?' Purrington demanded. 'This man's badly hurt. Help me get him to a doctor!'

Half a dozen men lifted Garza and, with Purrington striding beside them, carried him across the street to a doctor's office opposite the bank. As they reached the office the physician swung the door wide and stepped back to let them enter.

'Bring him back here,' the doctor directed.

'On that table. Now, give me some room!' He bent above Garza, looked at the welling blood and the glazed eyes, and then, stripping off his coat, went to work. Purrington stood by, watching anxiously. He heard movement, felt a hand touch his arm and, turning, stared into a seamed brown face.

'I'm the sheriff,' the newcomer announced. 'You're the man that did the shootin'. I want to talk to you.'

With a final reluctant glance at Garza, Purrington followed the sheriff out of the office.

Ruffin's Wild West gave no performance that afternoon. There was too much excitement in Willow Bluffs for anyone to attend so tame a thing as a Wild West show. Most of the performers and roustabouts went downtown, only a few remaining on the lot. Word filtered back to those who did not go, and when it was learned that Bugs Nixon and Tony Hart, two of the canvasmen, had been killed while trying to rob the Willow Bluffs Bank, there was considerable consternation. Three or four roustabouts waited to hear no more. They knew that the whole show would be investigated and pawed over by the law and, rolling their turkeys, they quietly slipped away. They were men who could not bear investigation.

Tom Ruffin, Purrington, Ruffin's lawyer, the fixer, all stayed in town, closeted with the

192

officials. When suppertime came and those who had gone to town came back to the lot, there was a great deal of talk, and as they sat down to the table in the cookhouse Ruffin and the sheriff appeared.

Ruffin made an announcement. 'I want everybody to go over to the big top. Right now.'

Cooks and canvasmen, hostlers, arena attendants, performers, all filed slowly to the big top. They noticed, as they walked, that hard-faced natives watched them. The sheriff had impressed a crew of deputies, and when the show people were assembled in the big tent the deputies guarded the doors.

Every person connected with the show was questioned as to his whereabouts during the bank robbery. Fortunately the show people had gone to town in groups, and every statement was substantiated by another. Nevada, questioned, said that she had been with Dan when the bank was held up, and Dan corroborated her. He said that he had run toward the bank when he heard the shooting, had seen the bandits, and that he and Nevada had been in the entry next to the store. There was no reason, as Dan saw it, to mention his having pulled Fatso out from under the mules.

'This is the man I told you about,' Ruffin informed the sheriff as the officer finished his questioning. 'The one that was attacked. Did you recognize either of the men, Dan?'

'No. Except Fatso.'

'Fatso,' Ruffin said gravely, 'is a Pinkerton detective.'

Dan's eyes widened at the information. The sheriff said: 'I want you to go downtown an' see if you know those fellows that were killed. See if they were the ones that attacked you.'

There was nothing that Dan could do but agree. Accompanied by a deputy, he left the big top.

Looking at Bugs's bullet-marked body at the undertaker's establishment, Dan shuddered. The undertaker spoke cheerfully. 'This one,' he said, indicating Tony, 'got hurt pretty bad a while back. Somebody kicked him in the groin.'

That clinched it for Dan. He remembered how he had used his knee during the battle and, turning to the deputy, said: 'These are the two, all right. I know now.'

The deputy wanted to know how Dan could be sure, and he grinned grimly when Dan answered.

'Well,' the deputy drawled when Dan had finished talking, 'yo're even with 'em. Let's go back.'

The officer was in good spirits as he accompanied Dan back to the lot. The story of the robbery tallied in detail with the robbery in Brule: The three men entered the bank just at noon; the people in the bank had been forced to lie face down on the floor, and the cashier was ordered to take the leader to the vault.

'Only he had a gun layin' under the teller's window,' the deputy stated, 'an' he grabbed it an' went to shootin'. He ducked down behind a desk an' was makin' it hot for 'em, an' they pulled out. An' that was when Purrington got 'em. Say, he's some shot, that boy is. He was standin' in a wagon an' the horses tryin' to get loose, an' he cut down three times. Killed both them fellers and would of got the third except that the team finally got loose an' jerked the wagon out from under him.'

'Where is the captain?' Dan asked.

'He's stayin' with that detective feller. That man's hurt bad. He was shot through a lung, an' a mule must of kicked his head. Looks like he'd make a die of it.'

When Dan and his companion reached the lot they found much excitement. A dragnet had been spread for the missing roustabouts, and the district attorney and deputy were still at their questioning.

Dan, making his report, announced that he had identified the dead men. The attorney nodded wisely and told Dan that he could go, but admonished him not to leave the lot. Dan left the tent wondering what good it did to have him say definitely that Bugs and Tony were his attackers.

The questioning continued until after midnight. Those that were released from the big top did not go to bed but waited for the others. It was almost three o'clock before the cars quieted and weary, excited people sought their beds. Dan, undressing, looked down at his chest as he always did to see the small gold saddle dangling there. The saddle was gone but the broken cord was still about his neck. He searched the floor beneath his bunk and the bunk itself, but the saddle was nowhere to be found. Somewhere he had lost it and, angry because he had not protected Penny's gift, Dan gave up the search.

*   *   *

Ruffin's Wild West stayed in Willow Bluffs another day. Dan was called as a witness at the inquest and listened to Captain Purrington's story. He watched the gray-eyed, grave-faced man as he talked, and marveled that the captain was unshaken. Dan listened, too, as Purrington gave an account of his acquaintance with Garza, heard the captain's slow drawl as he informed the coroner of a connection with the Rangers in Texas.

'I was a sergeant under Captain McDonald,' Purrington stated. 'I met Garza when we were working on some trouble in Ashleyville. That was when I first knew him.'

Finally the inquest was over. The jury filed out and returned with a verdict. The two dead men, the jury agreed, had met their fate while engaged in a crime of violence, and at the

196

hands of Captain Jack Purrington. The captain was to be complimented on his shooting.

When the inquest was finished Dan left the building with Ruffin. 'Now what?' he questioned.

'Now we'll get out of this town,' Ruffin growled. 'Of all the tough luck! First the blowdown an' then this! I'd sell the whole damned show for two bits.'

'What about the captain?' Dan asked. 'Will he go?'

'No,' Ruffin growled. 'He wants to stay here awhile until somebody comes to look after Garza.'

'An' what about Garza?'

'He hasn't recovered consciousness. The doctor gives him a fifty-fifty chance to live.'

For a time Dan and Ruffin walked in silence, then the showman voiced his thoughts. 'All that money right on the lot,' he rasped. 'You knew they'd found a pile of dough, didn't you? Found it in a couple of old grips that Bugs an' Tony had hid in a stock car. Think of it! All that money, an' me hard up as hell!'

CHAPTER FOURTEEN

The commercial house, Willow Bluffs' one hotel, was two stories high and faced the square. Emil Garza, occupying a room on the

197

second floor, could sit in his chair and, looking out the window, see the life of the little town as it circulated about the courthouse. He could see the trees too, and they were his calendar. For three weeks after he was shot he stayed in the town's small hospital, then, weak but definitely sure of recovery, he had been moved to his room. Prone in bed, he had watched the trees turn from green to a faint yellow, then to the full gold of frost-touched leaves. Now, in his chair, he watched the leaves come down, saw them make bronze wind-rows on the courthouse lawn as the bare skeletons of the trees appeared.

The man sent down from the New York office was gone, no longer needed. Garza was up and dressed and, weak as a newborn kitten, able to walk short distances about his room. In a few more days, a week perhaps, he would leave Willow Bluffs, and for that he was glad. The town was friendly and pleasant, but he had a distaste for it, regarding the place as a scene of failure. Idly he reached out to the table beside him and picked up a little pile of letters. Each bore a different cancelation, the names of the towns from which they had been mailed, marching in steady procession across the country north and west. Purrington had written regularly, expecting no answer save an occasional note detailing Garza's recovery. Garza opened the last letter and read it through.

DEAR EMIL, Purrington had written, *We are playing the last few stands this week, then will close the show at Lincoln. From there we go to Omaha, where we break up. I will be glad to see the close of the season, as will all the rest. Since leaving Willow Bluffs we have played to good crowds and done well, but I believe Ruffin is worried concerning financial matters and I know these last few weeks have been trying ones for us all.*

I see by your last letter that you expect to leave for New York soon, and that is indeed good news. I am glad that you are so completely recovered. Gunshot wounds, in my experience, are hard things to get over, and I have had a few. You say that you will have no ill effects, and that is good too, for very often a man may be crippled for life, particularly if he suffers a broken bone. In this cold weather we are having I notice that my old wound aches and bothers me considerably. I hope that this will not be true of you.

In your last letter you ask concerning Dan Mar. Mar is doing very well, but I do not believe that he is particularly happy. He seems to have something on his mind, and while I have tried to talk with him, I have not had much success. There is a general rumor among us that he and Nevada Warren are to be married after the show closes, but he does not act like a happily betrothed man. I still cannot see why you suspected Mar in the matter of the robberies. As I told you at the time, I thought that you were barking up the wrong tree. You were very close-mouthed about your reasons and now have been proven wrong. The two men killed in Willow Bluffs were definitely the men who attacked Mar, and if he had been their accomplice that would not have happened. One of those men who disappeared at the time of the robbery must have been the third party. You wrote that they have not been apprehended, but they will be in time, and then the whole mystery will be cleared up.

A few of us are going to winter at Ruffin's ranch, as in years past. I hope that you will write to me there. It would be a shame if we lost touch with each other again.

Let me hear from you when you get to New York, and if you can come out this winter. This would be a good place to finish recuperating, and I know that all would be glad to see you.

Your friend,

J. A. PURRINGTON

Garza laid the letter aside and stared at the window, not seeing the scene beyond the glass. Purrington was a good friend, a good man, but Garza wished that he had not shot so well. Garza was dissatisfied, uselessly so, he told himself. The case was wound up and a large part of the stolen money recovered. That should satisfy any man, but it did not. The

200

loose ends that remained, the missing third man and the unrecovered money, were bad enough, but more than these was the fact that Garza's reasoning had been faulty. He smiled sardonically as he thought of how he had erred. Three men with Ruffin's Wild West had committed the robberies and the murder, and of these, two were dead and the third a fugitive, hunted in every state of the Union. It was too bad, Garza thought, that Purrington had shot so well. Had he not been so deadly accurate, either Bugs Nixon or Tony Hart might have lived long enough to name their accomplice. Still Garza could not blame the captain for shooting straight. It was Purrington's business to hit a mark, and by straight shooting he had in all likelihood saved Garza's life. Another shot from Nixon's gun, Garza told himself grimly, might have done the business.

But how, he asked himself, could he have been so far wrong? The evidence pointed to Dan Mar: the missing mask, the fact that Mar was in the stage-holdup spectacle, that he had lost the mask, all those things pointed straight and true. He was slipping, Garza thought. Perhaps he had no business in returning to New York and to work again. Perhaps he would be better off in some other work. He had failed in this case, surely, and . . .

A knock sounded on the door and, without turning, Garza called, 'Come in.'

The hotel owner spoke from the door. 'There's some folks here to see you, Mr.

Garza.'

'Send them in.' Garza squared the chair around until it faced the door. A woman and a small boy, bashful and frightened, occupied the opening.

'Won't you come in?' Garza asked. 'You'll excuse me for not getting up, I know. I'm still pretty weak.'

Woman and boy entered, and the woman took a seat on the edge of a straight-backed chair while the boy hid behind her. 'You're that detective feller from New Yawk?' the woman asked.

Garza nodded.

'I'm Missus Coolman from out at Big Pinery.' Plainly the woman was uneasy. 'This yere's my boy Jimmy.'

'And what can I do for you?' Garza asked, smiling.

'Well'—Mrs. Coolman worked her hands nervously, pulling at her fingers—'it ain't what you can do for me, exactly. Show him, Jimmy.'

Jimmy lowered his head and said, 'Aw … Maw…'

'Well, then, I'll tell you. I reckon I'd have to anyhow. Yesterday Jimmy as foolin' around the house an' I asked him what he was a-doin'. He's always triflin' aroun', playin' cowboy an' such, ever since last summer when we come to town to see the show. He was a-playin', an' when I seen what he had I knowed it wasn't his. Give it to the gentleman, Jimmy.'

'Aw ... Maw ...'

'Give it yere then!' Mrs. Coolman half turned and seized her squirming offspring. Jimmy struggled briefly and then wailed.

'It's mine! I found it!'

A trifle red-faced, but triumphant, Mrs. Coolman held out her hand. On it lay a small replica of a saddle, made of gold, with silver stirrups and much fancy filigree work.

'This yere's what he had!' she said. 'He'd found it right on the bank corner the day the bank was robbed. I thought mebbe it would be some good to you.'

Garza took the saddle. 'Indeed it is,' he said, his eyes lighting. 'Indeed it is. Here, Jimmy!' He reached into his pocket and withdrew a silver dollar.

Jimmy, urged forward by his mother, advanced a halting step and snatched the dollar. 'Thank the gentleman, Jimmy,' Mrs. Coolman admonished.

Jimmy retreated behind the chair once more.

'He found it by the bank?' Garza asked. 'On the day of the robbery?'

'That's right, mister.' Mrs. Coolman stood up.

'Wait a minute,' Garza ordered. 'This is worth a good deal to me. I'd like to give you something. A reward ...'

'The Coolmans are good honest folks,' Mrs. Coolman said with pride. 'We don't want no reward. When I seen that an' learned where

Jimmy'd got it, I made Sam hitch right up an' bring me to town.'

'But ...' Garza expostulated.

Mrs. Coolman was plainly ready to go. 'You're welcome, mister,' she said. 'I knew that was a valuable thing an' I wanted to see it got into the right hands. Come on, Jimmy.'

Garza got up and followed the woman and boy to the door, speaking his thanks, still insisting that some reward was due.

Mrs. Coolman would have none of it. 'I only done what's right,' she announced at the door. 'Good-by, mister.'

Garza returned to his chair and sat down. The little gold saddle lay in his palm and, reversing it, he read the name engraved on the back: CARL THWAITE.

For a long time the man remained motionless, staring at that name, remembering the saddle fastened in Purrington's medal case, remembering Purrington's words: 'I wouldn't part with mine, and I don't think Ruffin or Darnell would give theirs away. Penny gave Carl's saddle to Dan Mar, and I know he means to keep it.'

Carefully, as though it were very precious, Garza put the saddle in a pocket of his vest. He had been right all the time; his reasoning had been correct. There were no more loose ends to fret him, no more unfinished business, and when he left Willow Bluffs he would not go east to New York but west to Brule. Garza's eyes gleamed his satisfaction and his jaw was square and firm. In one way and in only one way could that saddle have come to be by the bank. The third man, the sole remaining member of the murderous trio, was Dan Mar.

*　　*　　*

From Willow Bluffs, Ruffin's Wild West moved steadily across country. Five days after leaving the little town Captain Purrington rejoined the show. Purrington was uncommunicative when questioned concerning the happenings at the county-seat town, and it was evident that his role there had been distasteful. He was so pointed in his terseness that after a few attempts no one tried to get him to talk. On only one subject would the captain speak at all, and that was Emil Garza. Garza, the captain said, would get well, and a man had come down from the Pinkerton Agency to be with him and to clean up the loose ends of the case.

One other thing the captain said: The third man was still missing. The roustabouts who had run away from the show were being hunted and notices were being broadcast over the whole country. So far they had not been found. Purrington, Garza, the Willow Bluffs sheriff, every law officer connected with the case, thought that the third man was one of those missing roustabouts.

'Now,' Ruffin said, having listened to Purrington's brief report, 'maybe I can run a Wild West show an' not a detective agency. Maybe we can get along for the rest of the season without more trouble.'

It seemed that Ruffin's words were prophetic. The show went on toward the West, traveling across Oklahoma and up into Kansas. Days grew shorter and nights grew longer and colder. The last performance was played, and the red cars with the big yellow letters rolled to a stop in the Omaha yards.

Omaha was a breakup point. Ruffin paid off, and roustabouts went on one final drunk together. Performers made arrangements to transport personal possessions and stock to their winter quarters, shook hands with each other, and separated with many a 'write me this winter' or 'see you next season.' Only a little group remained with the cars: Ruffin, Kerr, a few hostlers to look after the stock, Penny, Dan Mar, Nevada, and Purrington.

The Darnells stayed in Omaha, as did Bob White, Red Halsey, and Shorty Thoms. The three men would come to the ranch later, Red told them, after their money was spent. Vainly he urged Dan to stay with them in Omaha. The Darnells did not plan to stay at the ranch during the winter, as they had done in years before, but Smokey told Ruffin that they would come up later to get their clothes and such other articles as they had left in the cottage at the ranch. All arrangements were made, and for the last trip of the season the red cars rolled out of the Omaha yards and on toward Brule.

In Brule the property cars were cut off and put on a siding. The stock cars were to go to Tejon, and while they waited Dan had time to go uptown. He visited the sheriff's office but found that Murrah had taken a prisoner to the penitentiary and had not yet returned.

'I'll come back and see him,' Dan told the office deputy. 'I'll be up at Ruffin's if he wants to talk to me.'

The deputy was plainly puzzled over the message, but Dan forestalled his questions by leaving the office. At the depot Dan found the others waiting, and at four o'clock they boarded the local passenger for Tejon. Dan settled Nevada in a seat, sat down himself, and leaned back wearily as the train began to move. They passed slowly through the yards and, looking out the window, Dan saw again the red sides of Ruffin's cars on the storage track. Carl Thwaite came into Dan's mind and the thing that Carl had said on just such an occasion. Dan could understand Carl now, could see why Carl hated the red cars and what they signified. Up ahead Penny sat beside Captain Purrington; Dan could see her yellow head above the top of the seat.

'It's good to be goin' home,' Dan said.

'We both need a vacation.' Nevada smiled at

her companion. 'A week or two at Tom's will do us good.'

'A week or two?' Dan looked down in surprise.

Nevada's head was turned toward the window. 'I've some letters out,' she answered casually. 'We ought to have a lineup for this winter by that time.'

Dan said nothing and, glancing up at him, Nevada continued. 'We've got a lot of things to do,' she said, 'and we've got a lot to talk over.'

'Yeah,' Dan agreed, without enthusiasm.

Beyond the window brown range country was sliding past. The engine whistled, two long and two short, and as the car passed the crossing Dan saw a man in a buckboard, holding a team of young horses that fought their heads.

'There's Barney Danning!' he exclaimed. 'I wonder why he's goin' to Brule.'

Nevada laughed. 'Local boy comes home!' she said.

The train stopped at Tejon, and, taking his own and Nevada's grips, Dan followed the girl to the platform. Young Buck Ruffin had brought the carryall and was waiting at the end of the platform.

'Put 'em in the back,' Buck directed. 'How are you, Dad? Hello, Dan. Hello, Nevada.' Buck shook hands all around, his brown face smiling, his eyes bright with his welcome. Ruffin got into the front seat and took the lines while Dan helped Penny and Nevada.

'Your folks are in town, Dan,' Buck informed. 'I saw 'em when I drove in.'

Dan climbed up beside Nevada, and Ruffin, all his passengers loaded, clucked to the team.

Rolling along Tejon's single street, Dan saw the MY buggy standing in front of a store, his mother on the seat.

'Stop a minute, Tom,' Dan called to Ruffin, and, jumping out over the still-turning wheel, ran to the buggy.

Clara Mar stood up and, as Dan reached her, stepped out of the buggy, light as a girl, into Dan's waiting arms. The greeting was wordless. Dan's arms were around his mother and her hungry arms held him tight. Then, having kissed her son, the woman held Dan at arm's length and looked at him through her tears. 'You're bigger, Danny,' she said. 'My, how you've grown! You're all right, son?'

'Sure, I'm all right. How are you, Mother? How have you been? It's sure good to be home.'

'It's good to have you home, Danny. So good!'

Ruffin had stopped the carryall and was looking back. Dan, holding his mother in a bear hug, could see Ruffin's impatience. 'I'm keepin' Tom waiting,' he said. 'I'll get my grip an' go home with you, Mother. I'll ...'

'Clara!'

Dan stepped back. Bruce Mar was on the

buggy seat, holding the lines. Dan was shocked to see his father's face. Bruce had aged woefully. His hair was grayer than Dan remembered, and the lines were deep carved about mouth and nose. Clara Mar turned when her husband called.

'I'm ready to go home,' Bruce said harshly. 'Come on!'

No word or sign of recognition to his son. Bruce Mar's eyes were as expressionless as though he looked at a stranger. Dan took an impulsive step toward the buggy. 'Dad!' he said.

'I don't know you!' Bruce rasped. 'Coming, Clara?'

For just an instant Clara Mar hesitated and then, obediently, went to the buggy. 'I'll see you, Dan,' she promised. 'Soon, son.'

She mounted the step and seated herself beside her husband. Bruce backed the buggy into the street, straightened it, and drove toward the west, and Dan, standing there, followed the course of the vehicle with his eyes. Clara looked back and lifted her hand, but Bruce, back humped over the lines, did not turn his head. After a moment Dan walked back to the waiting carryall and climbed in.

'Sorry I kept you waiting, Tom,' he said hoarsely.

CHAPTER FIFTEEN

The show stock came into Tejon the day after the performers arrived. Dan had spent a silent, moody evening, staying clear of all the rest, taking no part in their conversation, and they wisely left him alone. The next morning he went with Ruffin in the wagon, and on the way to town Ruffin broached the subject uppermost in Dan's mind.

'Bruce was kind of rough on you,' Ruffin growled, staring at the backs of his trotting team. 'I was afraid it would be that way. Are you goin' over to the MY?'

'I'm goin' to see Mother,' Dan answered quietly. 'I don't know whether I'll go to the ranch or not.'

'Bruce looks bad.' Ruffin kept his eyes on the horses. 'He's aged a lot. I'll talk to him an' try to fix things up.'

'Not on my account!' Dan's voice was iron-hard. 'I'll try to get along with Bruce, but he's got to make the first move. All I hate about it is that it's hard on Mother.'

'Women generally get the rough edge of the rock,' Ruffin stated.

For some time the only sound was that of the trotting horses. Ruffin turned his head. 'When are you an' Nevada goin' to hitch up?' he asked abruptly.

211

'Why ...' Dan equivocated, 'we haven't talked about that yet.'

'You'd better talk about it!' The showman's voice was harsh. 'I think a lot of Nevada. You'd better treat her right, Dan!'

Antagonism rose in Dan. 'Who said I wouldn't treat her right?' he rasped.

'Nobody.' Again the stillness broken by the steady purr of wagon wheels and the hoofbeats of the horses. 'You could be married at the ranch.'

'Maybe,' Dan drawled, 'we'd better let Nevada say what she wants to do.'

'Yeah.'

There was no further conversation. Both men in the wagon were engrossed in thought. As they entered Tejon, Ruffin spoke again.

'There's the cars. Buck's already begun to unload. I'll just pull around by the boxcar an' we'll get the stuff out.'

Two ranch hands helped unload the trunks, chests, and other material and pile it in Ruffin's wagon. Dan took his saddle up to the stockyards, caught Nigger, and, with Buck, started the horses home. The horses drove readily enough, and Buck spoke to his companion.

'Goin' to winter with us, Dan?'

'I don't know. Maybe.'

'We're workin' the pastures,' Buck announced, 'gettin' ready to ship. How about givin' me a hand?'

212

Dan's eyes lighted. 'You bet I will!' he agreed.

As a result of that brief conversation, Dan went to work with the ranch hands the next morning. Buck was rounding up the pastures, working the cattle for beef and redistributing his herd. It was nice work, good cow work, and it took time. The steers to be sold, and those heifers which Buck did not want to keep, went into one pasture. Other heifers, two-year-olds which were to be kept and bred, were cut out and put into another pasture. Dry cows, old bulls, lump jaws, cancer eyes, all the cull stock were separated and held.

Buck Ruffin ran the ranch just as a bookkeeper might keep books. He separated his cattle, each herd in its proper pasture, just as a bookkeeper enters income and expense items, each on its proper page in a ledger. Buck was a good cowman, none better, and to work with him was both an education and a pleasure. Dan said as much.

Buck's eyes were keen as he looked at his friend. 'If you like cattle so well, why don't you follow 'em?' he asked. 'Why do you stick in the show business?'

'To get a start,' Dan answered. 'You've got to have money before you can have an outfit.'

'How much money did you save this year?'

Dan grinned ruefully. 'Not any,' he admitted. 'You see, I had to buy all my outfit, an' then ... well, I guess I just spent too much.'

213

They were riding slowly through a bunch of cattle as they talked—the two-year-old heifers that Buck had worked in the Turkey Mountain pastures. Buck was shaping up the bunch, making his final cut.

'Yeah,' he drawled, 'I know how that is. An' the next year you'll spend too much too, an' then the next year after that you'll need new tack. I've worked for Dad ever since I was a kid. He's paid me wages an' I've taken them in cows. I've got my brand on half of these.' Buck gestured to the heifers.

'You're lucky,' Dan said briefly. 'I never drew wages an' I haven't got a cow.'

'There's one that's got to come out,' Buck said. 'That mottle face. Get her, will you, Dan?'

Dan worked the mottle-faced heifer toward the edge of the herd, rancor filling him. Buck had a bunch of cattle and Dan Mar had none. Buck did the thing he wanted to do and, so Dan had discovered, the thing Dan Mar wanted to do. He gave the heifer a shove toward the cut, his horse working like a clock when the mottle face tried to break back.

'I'll get the money,' Dan said when he rejoined his friend. 'I'll get it some place, an' when I do I'll have an outfit.'

'You'll not get it in the show business,' Buck replied. 'I guess these are all right, Dan. You an' Frank take the cut down to the old bull pasture, will you?'

'Sure.'

With Frank helping, Dan moved the cut, a slow, long trip. Dusk had come when finally Dan and his companion reached the headquarters.

There was a buggy at the hitch rail in front of Ruffin's house and lights gleamed from the windows. In the dusk Dan could not be sure of the buggy at that distance, and his heart jumped to his throat. That buggy was, in all likelihood, from the MY. Perhaps his mother had driven over to see him.

'I'll be down in a minute,' Dan said and, leaving his companion, trotted his weary horse toward the house.

Disappointment awaited him. The buggy belonged to Tejon's storekeeper, and Dan turned to ride back to the corrals when Ruffin called him from the porch.

'Dan, is that you?'

'Yeah,' Dan answered.

'Come in here a minute.'

Dismounting, Dan wrapped the reins over the rail and went to the porch. Ruffin had gone in, for the air was cold with coming frost. Dan pushed open the door and walked into the living room.

Ruffin and Purrington were there, and Art Murrah, the sheriff. Instantly Dan thought that Murrah had come to see him in answer to the letter and the message left with the deputy. It was not until he was well into the room that he saw the fourth man seated in a big chair.

Dan faced the man.

'Hello, Garza,' he said. 'I thought you were still back in Willow Bluffs.'

'I was.' Emil Garza straightened himself. 'But I wanted to see you, Mar.'

'To see me?' Dan could not understand. 'What did you want to see me about?'

'Various things. The bank robbery at Willow Bluffs, for one.'

Dan shook his head. 'I thought that was all cleaned up,' he said.

'Not quite.'

'Dan!'

Dan turned to face the sheriff. 'Yes?'

Purrington and Ruffin looked at Dan as though he were a total stranger. Murrah held a paper in his hand. 'This is a warrant,' the sheriff announced. 'Yo're under arrest, an' I've got to tell you that anythin' you say can be used against you.'

'Me?' Dan could not believe that he had heard correctly. 'Under arrest?' Involuntarily his muscles tightened, bunching under his coat.

'He's goin' to make a break!' Garza warned sharply. 'Get the cuffs on him!'

'Put out yore hands!' Murrah snapped. 'Don't try it, Dan!'

Dan stood trembling like a colt that feels a rope for the first time. Cold metal touched his wrist. Garza was beside him, holding a pair of cuffs. At the touch of that cold steel Dan Mar exploded. His arm shot out, and Garza reeled

216

back. Murrah, dropping the warrant, reached for his gun. Dan was on him like a cat. Two swift blows sent the sheriff staggering, and with the way clear Dan jumped for the door, snatched it open, and was gone!

He was across the porch and down the steps before Murrah regained his feet. The sheriff lumbered to the door, fouled with Garza in the opening, and stuck there; and Dan, vaulting the hitch rail, caught the loosely wrapped reins, jerked them free, and swung up. His horse, frightened by the sudden movement, reared and pivoted, then, stung by stabbing spurs, jumped his full length and lit running.

Murrah crowded past Garza and flung a futile shot after the running horse. Dusk was merging into night, and into the darkness horse and rider disappeared. As the reverberations of the shot died the pound of rapid hoofbeats came back to the men on the porch. Murrah holstered the gun and swung around to face the others outlined in the light from the open door.

'By God!' he rasped. 'I'll get him. I'll get that boy if it's the last thing I do!'

Buck Ruffin and the riders, alarmed by the shot, came running from the bunkhouse, shouting questions as they came. Murrah glared at Purrington and Ruffin. 'Why didn't you stop him?' he demanded. 'You could have done it!'

'I didn't ...' Ruffin began.

Purrington, quiet and coldly scornful,

interrupted. 'The only way I could have stopped him was with a gun. I didn't want to kill him. You damned fools, why did you try to put cuffs on him? He'd have stood still and answered questions. Why didn't you tell Tom and me that you had a warrant instead of saying you wanted to question him?'

'Yo're his friends!' Murrah snapped. 'If I'd told you I had a warrant you'd of let it slip.'

Purrington laughed mirthlessly. 'It seems to me *you* let things slip. Dan's gone. You said you wanted to question him about that robbery in Willow Bluffs. It'll be some time before you ask him questions now!'

Buck and his cowhands had arrived and were babbling questions. Penny and Nevada had come out on the porch. Murrah glared about him. 'Get inside!' he ordered. 'We've got things to do. Come on!'

In the living room Garza consulted with the sheriff. Purrington talked to Penny and Nevada, telling them what had happened, and Ruffin answered the questions that his son and the others poured out.

'It's a confession of guilt,' Garza said again. 'He admitted he was guilty when he ran.'

'Of robbing the bank at Willow Bluffs?' Nevada's scornful voice broke through a babel of sound, and Garza turned to face her. Nevada looked contemptuously at the Pinkerton man. 'Dan Mar,' she said, 'pulled you out from under a bunch of mules at Willow

Bluffs. That's the reason you're alive. I saw him do it. I was in the store next to the bank and I made Dan take me back to the lot.'

'Mar pulled me out?' Garza stared at Nevada. 'Why didn't you tell me?'

'You didn't ask me,' Nevada answered scornfully. 'You came in and shooed Penny and me out of the room as though we were children!'

'It makes no difference what he did!' Murrah rasped. 'He resisted arrest an' got away, an' I'm goin' to get him. Buck, you take a telegram down to Tejon right now. We'll organize a posse an' go after him, an' I want my deputies to know what's happened. I want a net spread for Mar. Garza, you go down to the bunkhouse an' search Mar's grip an' trunk. I'm goin' to the MY. He might head for there. Now let's get goin'.'

Under the sheriff's orders, work began. Garza went to the bunkhouse, while Murrah wrote a telegram to his chief deputy in Brule. Buck, expostulating, saddled a fresh horse to carry the message in to Tejon. Before he left, Garza came back from the bunkhouse.

'Not much,' he answered when Murrah asked him what he had found. 'There was an envelope with some money in it an' another envelope with a ten-dollar bill.'

'Let's see.' Murrah held out his hand.

'That ten dollars is part of Dan's first salary after we began the act,' Nevada drawled.

Murrah paid no attention. He was looking at five crisp new twenty-dollar bills spread before him on the table. Drawing a list from his pocket, he compared the serial numbers of the bills with those on the paper. When he looked up his voice was triumphant. 'Maybe Mar didn't have a hand in the job at Willow Bluffs. I don't care if he did or not. He's wanted right here now, not back in Missouri.'

'What do you mean?' Ruffin asked.

'I mean that these bills were in his grip an' that they came from the Stockman's robbery. That's what I mean. The numbers are on this list.'

They clustered about the sheriff, Ruffin and Purrington peering over his shoulders, the others trying to see. Murrah's blunt forefinger followed a penciled line of figures and his voice rasped: 'D 65233457 C, D 65233458 C, D 65233459 C ... Is that enough?' Still the harsh triumph rang in his voice. About him Nevada and Penny, Purrington and Ruffin, and all the rest looked questioningly at each other.

'An' now'—the sheriff pushed himself up from the table—'let's get goin'. Here's the telegram, Buck. You take it to Tejon. An' the rest of you men come with me. Yo're my deputies. We'll go to the MY.'

*　　　*　　　*

Dan Mar, when he threw Garza aside and

struck Murrah, acted instinctively. He was not afraid, and he did not reason or think out his acts. He reacted to the touch of cold steel against his wrist as instinctively as a bronco that first feels a cold saddle on his back. Like the horse, Dan bucked and fought for freedom. That swift, instinctive action gained it for him. He was away, across the porch and on his horse, almost before the slower, methodical minds of the others could realize what had happened. He heard the roar of the shot that followed him, but the lead came nowhere near. Darkness engulfed him, and, his eyes still blinded by the lights in Ruffin's living room, he let the horse run. They went crashing away toward the east, dropped into the draw beyond the house, and came scrambling up the other side. For a mile Dan's horse held the mad run and then, weary from a day's work, the animal slowed. Dan spurred, and again his mount responded, only to slow again.

Now reason began to return, and with it hot anger. Murrah had arrested him, for what reason Dan did not know. Garza had tried to handcuff him and had failed, just as Murrah's arrest had missed fire. He was a fugitive. Dan reined in his horse and listened intently. He heard nothing, no sound of pursuit, nothing but the little noises in the quiet night. His horse pulled against the reins and took a few tentative steps back toward headquarters. Dan checked the movement. Where, he asked

221

himself, should he go? Not back to Ruffin's, surely. Not back to those handcuffs and those strange, staring eyes. To the MY? No, not there. He could not ride in and tell Bruce what had happened. The MY was not his home. Where, then?

Deliberately Dan thought it over. His eyes were accustomed to the night now, and in the starlight he could see the bulk of Turkey Mountain looming above the northern horizon. His question was answered. He turned his mount toward the north and, without hurry, rode toward Turkey Mountain and the roughs of Vinegar Creek beyond. A modicum of safety waited him there. In that rough country he could hide, could dodge those that were sure to come after him. Time enough to decide what to do after he had reached the roughs. Time enough to sit down and think it out then. The horse stumbled, and Dan pulled him up sharply. The way was long to the rough country, and he had a tired horse.

At midnight, or so the stars told him, Dan passed Turkey Mountain and went through the gate in Ruffin's north fence. There would be trackers among the men who followed him, and, remembering that, Dan had chosen his path with care. He cut through the spot where during the day he had worked cattle with Buck Ruffin, knowing that the horse tracks would be confusing and that his pursuers would have difficulty in singling out his line of flight.

Beyond that spot he forced his weary horse to climb a long rocky ridge, cutting back on his trail a time or two as he would have done had he been handling cattle. Then, believing that the trail was confused enough, he struck out for the gate.

Beyond the gate Dan followed down a draw until, reaching the seeps that formed the head of Vinegar Creek, he stopped and let his horse water. That done, he went down the draw, keeping in the creek for almost half a mile. Satisfied that he had confused any pursuit, he pulled out of the water and continued his way. The broken country welcomed him, and he entered it and stopped. Here, where little draws choked with buckbrush and squawberry beset the country, he was safe for a while.

Making a stake rope of his whale line, Dan removed his bridle and, having loosened the cinch, picketed his horse. Then, while the breeze rustled the buckbrush, he sought a little canyon and, sitting down, stared gloomily at the stars. He was weary, with a bone-aching weariness. He was hungry and he was cold. The stars crawled by overhead, changing position minutely. The wind whimpered above the draw. The horse, in better case than its rider, tore coarse grass from the bunches between the brush and munched it, and Dan Mar waited for the dawn.

CHAPTER SIXTEEN

Murrah came stamping into Ruffin's living room, slammed down his hat, and scowled at Emil Garza. 'He wasn't there,' the sheriff rasped. 'Hadn't been there. I'd just as soon run into a nest of rattlesnakes as Bruce Mar when he's on the prod!'

The sheriff seated himself ponderously on a chair. On the porch Ruffin's voice sounded as he gave directions to Buck; and Purrington, coming in quietly, closed the door. It was midnight, and Dan Mar had been gone for five hours.

'I take it,' Garza said, 'that Mr. Mar resented what you had to say about his son?'

'Resented it?' Murrah laughed harshly and without mirth. 'He all but jumped down my throat. I left a man over there to watch for Dan, but I don't think he'll go to the MY.'

'Why not?' Garza, because of his weakness, had not ridden with the sheriff.

'Because,' Purrington explained. 'Dan and his father are at outs. Bruce didn't want Dan to go with Ruffin's show this year.'

Tom Ruffin came in and dropped into a chair. 'Now what?' he asked. 'Have you any more fool ridin' to do, or can we go to bed, Art?'

Murrah scowled at Ruffin. 'Go to bed if you

want to,' he growled. 'You'll ride plenty tomorrow.'

'I'll ride nowhere tomorrow,' Ruffin snapped. 'You can get yore own deputies to do yore ridin'.' He leaned back in the chair and relaxed, eying the sheriff.

Garza shifted in his chair and, producing the little gold saddle, examined it again. 'My case against Mar isn't as good as it was a few hours back,' he said ruefully.

'What do you mean?' Murrah glared at the Pinkerton man.

Garza shrugged and toyed with the saddle. 'I told you how I got this. Miss Warren says that Mar pulled me out from beneath a bunch of mules. He might have dropped his watch charm then. I was basing my case on this charm and the masks.'

'Maybe yore case is no good,' Murrah snapped, 'but mine is all right. That money in Dan's grip came from the Stockman's Bank. An' he as good as said he was guilty when he ran!'

Silence filled the room as the men sat, thinking moodily. A door creaked, and every eye turned toward the sound. Penny, Nevada following her, came into the living room.

'You didn't find Dan?' Nevada drawled.

'No.' Ruffin shook his head. 'He hadn't gone to the MY.'

'Where did you get that?' Penny's voice was strained as she advanced a step and pointed to the saddle Garza held. 'That's Carl's.'

'It was found and given to me.' Garza looked up at the girl. 'Why?'

'I gave it to Dan. Did he lose it?'

Garza nodded. 'He lost it. Why did you give it to him, Miss Thwaite?'

'Because ...' Penny said, and then with a rush: 'Because I'd told him he was to blame for Carl's being killed. It wasn't so. I wanted to give Dan something of Carl's to show Dan I didn't mean what I'd said. He and Carl had quarreled, and Dan rode away and ... I gave him the saddle to show that there were no hard feelings, that everything was all right.'

'Mar and your brother quarreled, you say?' Garza's voice was gentle. 'About what, Miss Thwaite?'

'Because Carl wouldn't take him in our act. They almost fought, and I stopped them. Dan rode off and he wouldn't come back when Carl called him. And then Carl was killed and ... Give it to me, please. It belongs to me.'

Garza placed the saddle in Penny's outstretched hand and, clutching it, the girl turned blindly and went to the door, Nevada following her. At the door Nevada stopped.

'I hope you're satisfied!' she snapped. 'You've made her cry!' The door banged shut behind Nevada's indignant back.

'It seems to me,' Ruffin said heavily, 'that there was no need of that, Garza. You just made the girl feel bad.'

226

Garza stared moodily at the floor. 'How was Thwaite killed?' he asked suddenly.

'Horse fell on him,' Ruffin answered.

'Who found him?'

'Penny. Carl left her, an' when he didn't come back she went to look for him. Why?'

'Just thinking,' Garza drawled. 'What was the coroner's verdict in Thwaite's death?'

'I told you!' Ruffin's voice was angry. 'His horse fell an' killed him. He'd been dragged an' kicked. His head was all stove in.'

'Was there an autopsy?'

Murrah answered that question. 'No. Why do you ask that?'

'Because,' Garza drawled, 'this whole thing, this series of crimes, the robbery of the Brule bank, all of them tie up right here at Ruffin's winter quarters. Thwaite was a good rider, wasn't he? He wasn't a man to be easily thrown?'

'You don't have to be thrown when yore horse goes down!' Ruffin snapped. 'You take out after somethin' an' yore horse falls an', good rider or not, yo're lucky if you ain't killed.'

'Then Thwaite was chasin' something?'

Blank silence followed the question. Then Ruffin said: 'No, he wasn't. Red an' Dan got all the buffalo over west of Turkey Mountain.'

'And Mar and Thwaite had quarreled,' Garza reminded softly.

'Do you think Mar killed Carl?' Murrah

227

snapped. 'Is that what yo're drivin' at?'

Garza shook his head. 'Thwaite's horse may have fallen, just as you say. I don't know. I do know that an autopsy should have been performed. There should always be an autopsy when a man is violently killed.'

'If the undertaker had found anythin' wrong he'd have told me,' Murrah said slowly. 'I dunno ... It's not too late yet.'

'I think you two are crazy!' Ruffin snapped. 'I'm goin' to bed.'

Purrington got up and stretched. 'I'm inclined to agree with Tom,' he drawled. 'I think I'll go to bed too.'

'We'll start early!' Murrah warned.

'All right, we'll start early. I'll show you two where you can sleep.' Ruffin advanced toward the hall door. 'An' if you think yo're goin' to pull my men off their jobs in the mornin' an' send 'em all over the country lookin' for Dan, yo're mistaken.' Ruffin paused beside the door. 'We're gettin' ready to ship an' I need 'em.'

Murrah and Garza followed Ruffin. The sheriff had had enough of Ruffin's rasping. 'If you think I ain't goin' to use 'em,' he said levelly, 'yo're a lot more mistaken than I am. An' if you think you ain't goin' to ride in the posse you'd better change yore mind. I've sworn you in as a deputy, Tom, an' you'll do what I say. Now where's the bed?'

Ruffin put Garza and the sheriff in the same

room, and as they undressed Murrah spoke. 'Them two like Dan Mar. They don't think he's guilty, in spite of him runnin' away.'

'They're good men,' Garza answered, 'and good friends. Mar did run away, but maybe...'

'Maybe what?'

'Maybe he isn't guilty of bank robbery.'

Murrah ceased his preparations and stared at the Pinkerton man. 'Are you crawfishin'?' he demanded. 'You come out here an' get me to take out a warrant for Dan Mar an' tell me about the case you got an' all an' then you say he ain't guilty?'

'I said,' Garza spoke slowly, 'that perhaps he wasn't guilty of bank robbery. I didn't say he wasn't guilty.'

'Of what?'

'Dan Mar'—Garza slid into the bed and pulled up the covers—'is a mighty impulsive youngster. He does things quickly, on the spur of the moment, without thinking. He quarreled with Carl Thwaite. If I were you I'd order that autopsy, Murrah.'

Murrah paused, his hand behind the lamp chimney. The implications of what Garza had just said struck him and held him motionless. Then: 'I'll do that in the mornin',' he answered quietly. 'I'll wire the district attorney an' have him get a court order. Good night.' With a puff he blew out the lamp.

*   *   *

Dan Mar hunted rabbits. Equipped with a long forked stick, he prowled the buckbrush, up and down the little draws. When he startled a cottontail he ran, blundering through the brush, and sometimes the rabbit took to a hole. Then Dan reached into the hole with his stick, down and down, and perhaps prodded something soft. Twisting the stick, he caught it in the rabbit's fur and presently hauled out his wriggling, frightened prey. When this occurred, a blow with the back of his hand placed the touch of success upon his enterprise and he had rabbit to eat. In two days he had become woefully sick of cottontail as a steady diet.

Three times during the two days he had seen parties of horsemen riding the rough country along Vinegar Creek. Once he had hidden in a canyon, screened by high brush, and once he had mounted and slipped away, circling to come back behind the riders. The country was being systematically combed for him, and presently he knew that he must leave it.

How he left was a question of debate. Two days give plenty of time for thought, and Dan realized his predicament. By running away he had tacitly admitted guilt of whatever it was of which he was accused. He had been foolish to run away, and now he regretted it. He had done better to stay, face the music, find out why Murrah had taken out a warrant. He could, of course, go back and surrender himself and start over. But if he did that, he was in the hole. Whenever he thought of giving himself up he could feel again the touch of cold metal on his wrist and see once more the staring, curious eyes of Ruffin and Purrington and the rest, eyes that surveyed him as though he were a stranger.

On the other hand, there was a lot of country beyond Vinegar Creek and the roughs. Nothing prevented his seeking that country. The parties that sought him could follow his tracks, and he would be at the far end of those tracks, making more. The prospect intrigued Dan except for certain things. If he left the country, what would his mother think, and Penny? For that matter, what did they think now?

Brown fur blurred through the brush, and Dan flung a stone and followed after. The rabbit ducked into a hole, and Dan prodded carefully. Rewarded for his efforts, Dan killed the rabbit and carried it up the draw. There, where a red sandstone bluff came down, was a small pocket in which Dan's saddled horse grazed. Under the bluff was a cave, a minor niche in the sandstone. Dan broke dry wood as he walked toward his home and, under the niche, carefully uncovered a coal of oak. Fire was a problem, for there had been but eight matches in his pocket and now there were four. The little blaze, blown tenderly to life, crackled almost without smoke, and Dan, producing his knife, skinned and dressed the cotton-tail, eying it distastefully.

Having washed the rabbit in the creek, he was returning to the cave when he heard a horse coming gingerly over rock. He crouched in the brush and worked cautiously toward his own mount. Dan's horse was watching the ridge beside the bluff, ears cocked alertly, and Dan, following the direction of that look, saw a single horseman coming down into the pocket. He waited, motionless, and then, straightening, strode forward. The rider was Penny Thwaite.

Man and girl met below the bluff. Penny sat motionless as Dan came up, and neither spoke for a moment. Then Dan said: 'How did you know I was here, Penny?'

'This is where we played,' Penny answered simply. 'Remember, Dan?'

The man nodded and, placing his hand on a rein, led horse and rider toward the cave. Penny swung down and lifted a sack from her saddle while Dan tied the horse. When he returned Penny had opened her sack, displaying food, bread and meat, and a can that could contain nothing but coffee.

'I couldn't get away until this morning,' she said. 'They're looking for you. Murrah and all his deputies are staying at Ruffin's, but they didn't come back last night.'

Dan squatted down beside the opened sack. He had not known how hungry he was, but now, restraining his appetite, he divided the bread and sliced the chunk of beef.

'Dan,' Penny said.

The man looked up.

'You've got to get away.'

Dan waited. 'They think that you killed Carl,' Penny said, almost choking over her brother's name. 'Mr. Murrah got an order from the court. They ... they found a bullet in Carl's head.'

Dan did not move; he simply squatted there and stared unbelievingly at the girl. 'I came to tell you that you'll have to get away.' Penny rushed the words. 'Now! Right away, Dan.'

'They say I killed Carl?'

A wordless nodding.

'I didn't! You don't believe I did that, Penny?'

'No. I don't believe it. I've told them I don't. And I'm not going back to Ruffin's. I'm going to the MY. Your father doesn't believe it either, and your mother asked me to come.'

Dan got up. 'Is that why Murrah tried to arrest me?'

Penny shook her head. 'They thought that you'd been one of a gang that traveled with the show. They thought you were mixed up in a lot of robberies and a murder, but now they think that you killed Carl and that you robbed the Stockman's Bank.'

'Me?'

Penny nodded.

'But I ...' Dan began. Again there came the sound of a horse's cautious progress over rock. Penny's eyes were wide with fear, and she took the step that separated her from the man. Instinctively Dan's arms went about her, and for an instant they were together, each holding the other close. Then Penny shoved him away. 'Hide!' she whispered. 'I'll tell them you're not here. I'll take them away.'

Dan shook his head. 'I'll not let you!' His answer was fierce. 'No, Penny. I'll give up.'

In the draw Dan's horse nickered, and Penny's mount was staring toward the east. A horse came around the end of the sandstone, and Nevada Warren said tonelessly: 'I thought you'd be here.' She swung down lithely and walked forward, leading her mount.

'How did you ...?' Penny began.

'I thought you'd know where Dan was hiding,' Nevada said casually. 'I watched you and followed when you left. You two fool kids! Don't you know that this is dangerous? Why did you run away, Dan?'

Nevada seated herself on a boulder and stared at the two.

'I don't know,' Dan answered. 'I lost my head, I guess. They tried to put handcuffs on me, and when I felt them I just went haywire.'

Nevada continued to study Penny and Dan. 'You'd better come back and give yourself up,' she stated. 'You'll be caught if you don't. And if Smokey Darnell sees you first you'll be killed.

It would be the chance he's waiting for.'

Penny said 'No!' violently. 'Dan's going to get away.'

Dan said: 'Smokey Darnell?'

'He's back at Ruffin's,' Nevada drawled, 'and he's riding with the sheriff's posse. He'd like nothing better than a shot at you, Dan.'

'Dan's going to get away,' Penny repeated. 'He can go to Canada. I won't let him come back.'

'And have murder hanging over him the rest of his life?' Nevada shook her head. 'It won't do.'

'You want him caught!' Penny accused. 'You want him put in jail.'

'I want him to clear himself,' Nevada corrected firmly. 'You two kids haven't thought this thing out.'

Penny stepped away from Dan, watching Nevada narrowly. Dan, too, stared at the woman. Nevada laughed mirthlessly. 'Do you know what you're up against?' she demanded. 'Did Penny tell you what Murrah had found?'

Dan nodded.

Penny continued to stare at Nevada. 'You hate us both!' she accused. 'That's why you followed me here. You hate me and you hate Dan. Why didn't you bring the sheriff with you? Why didn't you bring Smokey and let him kill Dan? You ...' Penny's voice rose hysterically, and Dan reached out and touched her. Instinctively the girl turned to him.

'I don't hate you,' Nevada said wearily. 'Neither of you. It wouldn't have worked, Dan. I'm older than you are and we're a different kind of people. I've known that you were in love with Penny ever since the night of the blowdown. It's all right.'

His arm about Penny's shoulders, Dan automatically comforted the girl as he continued to stare at Nevada.

Once again Nevada laughed her harsh, mirthless laugh. 'You were high because we'd put on a good act and got a lot of applause,' she said. 'It had gone to your head. I knew that, Dan; I never took it seriously. I knew that you were in love with Penny and that she loved you.' Nevada would not meet Dan's steady eyes and turned her own away. 'And you thought you'd committed yourself,' she continued. 'You thought you had to go through with it. I never was in love with you. You're just a kid.'

Penny said: 'You mean you weren't in love with Dan at all? You mean...'

'There are no strings on Dan,' Nevada interrupted. 'That's all I mean.'

It seemed to Dan that Penny's arms tightened before she released him.

'And now that I've got that off my chest,' Nevada said, 'what about going back to Ruffin's? Your father's there, Dan, and he's fighting mad. He swears that Murrah will never catch you and that if he does he'll get the

236

best lawyer in the state and just turn things upside down.'

'Dad?' Dan said, bewildered.

'Your father. That man is certainly mad. He's jumped all over Murrah and Ruffin, and Garza too. He's on the warpath.'

Dan laughed. 'If Dad's on the prod, I wouldn't like to be Art Murrah,' he said happily.

'Dan,' Nevada said seriously, 'how did that money come to be in your grip?'

'What money? The only money I had in my grip was ten dollars from my first salary from the act and a hundred dollars that Smokey paid me on a bet.'

'Can you prove that?' Nevada came up from the boulder.

'Of course I can. Red saw me put it in there. And you know about the salary money. Why, Nevada?'

'Because that money was taken from the Stockman's Bank when it was robbed!'

It took an instant for Dan to assimilate the statement. He stared at Nevada. 'Then Smokey ...' he began.

'Red's not at the ranch,' Nevada warned. 'Smokey will say he didn't give it to you.'

'Then I'll find Red an' prove he did.'

'But,' Penny interposed, 'Mr. Murrah thinks that Dan killed Carl. Since they found that bullet he thinks ...' Penny broke off.

Dan's eyes were narrow. 'I can prove that I

didn't kill Carl too,' he drawled. 'I'll go in with you, Penny. Right away. I'll give myself up.'

CHAPTER SEVENTEEN

Garza played solitaire in the living room, the regular slap of the cards the only sound in all of Ruffin's big house. As he turned the cards he heard a horse arrive, the creak of leather as a man dismounted, and then boot heels thumping on the porch. Garza put the deck aside, and the door opened, admitting Bruce Mar.

'Well,' Bruce barked at the Pinkerton man, 'has Murrah come in yet?'

Garza shook his head. 'No. He didn't come back last night.'

Bruce removed his coat and unwrapped his neckcloth. 'An' if he don't come in till he finds Dan, he won't come at all,' the big man stated with satisfaction. 'Dan's too smart for him. Where's Penny?'

'She left this morning. She said that she was going to your place.'

'To my place?' Bruce came over to stand beside Garza's table. 'She didn't get there. Where's Nevada?'

Garza shrugged. 'She started out after Penny. Didn't you see them?'

'No.' Bruce sat down. 'They weren't at the

ranch; I just left there. Maybe they went to Tejon.'

'Maybe.' Garza picked up the deck again. 'But Penny said that she was going to visit Mrs. Mar.'

'You can play that red seven,' Bruce directed. 'When did Murrah say he'd be back?'

'Sometime today.' Garza played the red seven. 'I think he's coming now.' The regular sound of trotting horses filtered into the living room.

'That's him.' Bruce went to the window. 'An' he ain't got Dan.'

Boots thumped on the porch and Murrah swung open the door. He nodded to Bruce and scowled as he spoke to Garza.

'Must be nice to sit an' play cards. It beats ridin'.'

Garza folded the deck. He was a little tired of Murrah's rasping. 'I'd ride if I could,' the detective said briefly. 'Did you find anything?'

'No.' Murrah pulled off his coat and dropped it beside the table. 'I didn't. I'm goin' to call it off. We won't find Dan. He's left the country.'

Bruce Mar chuckled. 'You wouldn't find him if he'd stayed,' he assured. 'I told you that.'

Murrah's eyes were narrow as he turned to Bruce. 'Maybe yo're hidin' him.'

'Mebbe I am.'

Voices sounded from outside the house where the posse was breaking up. Ruffin said:

'I don't know; I'm not the boss here any more. Ask Murrah!'

The sheriff scowled at the door as Tom Ruffin came in, followed by his son and Purrington. Ruffin paused just inside the room. 'Have you had enough?' he demanded. 'Or are we goin' to keep up this foolishness?'

'I'm through lookin' here,' Murrah answered, 'but I won't quit huntin'. I won't need yore men any more.'

'An' *that's* good news,' Buck Ruffin said. 'Maybe we can deliver cattle now.'

'I don't care what you do now!' Murrah snapped. 'I'm goin' in to Brule tomorrow, but don't think I'm goin' to drop this. I'll get Dan.'

'Yeah,' Bruce drawled, 'just like you got him!'

'Damn you, Bruce!' Murrah wheeled on the older Mar. 'If yo're hidin' Dan I'll have you arrested for murder too. I think . . .'

'I think yo're crazy,' Bruce interrupted bluntly. 'Dan never killed Carl. An' if you think you can arrest me, try it! The only thing I'm sorry about is that Dan didn't knock yore fool head off when he got away. That's what he should of done!'

'Bruce!' Ruffin warned. 'Stop it!'

'Well, damn it! He's got no business accusin' my boy of murder!'

Ruffin walked over to his neighbor. 'You cool down,' he ordered. 'After all, Art's the sheriff an' he's got to do his duty.'

240

Bruce Mar subsided amid rumblings, and Murrah looked at Garza. 'Any telegrams come while we were gone?'

'No.' Garza was placing cards again. 'Nothing.'

'An' they won't.' The sheriff sat down beside Garza's table. 'I told you when we sent 'em we were wastin' money. Dan won't hit any towns.'

Buck Ruffin, going to the window, peered out at the gray afternoon. 'It looks like we'd quit just in time,' he drawled. 'It's goin' to snow. I wish we had our steers in the pens.'

'We would have if we hadn't been foolin' around,' Ruffin stated pointedly. 'Where's Smokey? I thought he was comin' in.'

'Belle called him. He went up to his house.' Buck pushed the window curtains aside. 'Here comes Nevada. Where has she been?'

'She and Penny went out this morning,' Garza informed. 'They said they were going to Mar's place, but he hasn't seen them.'

'If Penny's lost, that will be just fine!' Ruffin snapped. 'That's about all we need. Didn't she get to your place, Bruce?'

'No.'

The men waited. They heard a horse stop and steps mount the porch. Nevada entered the living room and, having surveyed the group, spoke. 'Do you want Dan Mar, Sheriff?'

'You know I do,' Murrah snapped. 'Have you seen him? Where is he?'

'Nevada!' Bruce warned. 'Don't you...'

241

Nevada interrupted. 'Sit down,' she said to Bruce. 'Dan's all right. I know where he is, and he'll give himself up if you'll promise one thing.'

'What's that?' Murrah demanded.

'You're not to put handcuffs on him.'

'No!' Bruce said again. 'I won't have it, Nevada.'

Nevada smiled wearily at the anxious man. 'It's all right, Mr. Mar,' she assured. 'Well, what about it, Sheriff?'

Murrah stood undecided. 'All right,' he agreed. 'I won't put the cuffs on him. Where is he?'

'I'll bring him in.' Nevada stepped out to the porch and, lifting her hat, waved it back and forth. The men crowded out after her, and from the draw beyond the house Dan Mar and Penny lifted themselves and rode slowly forward. 'Remember what you promised,' Nevada warned.

Before the two riders reached the house Bruce Mar ran down the steps. Murrah might have restrained him, but Bruce gave no warning of his intentions. Dan checked his horse, and Bruce stared up at his son. For an instant neither spoke, and then the older man said, 'Dan!' There was appeal in his voice, apprehension and anxiety. In that instant Dan was given his chance to avenge all the slights and neglects that had sent him away from the MY, his opportunity to repay the cold, hard

242

bitterness that Bruce had shown him. For a second Dan's eyes were hard, and Penny, reading them, caught her breath. Then Dan bent forward.

'Do you mean it, Dad?' he demanded.

Bruce Mar could not meet his son's eyes. He turned his head away, and his voice rasped chokingly. 'I wouldn't blame you if you told me to go to hell, the way I've treated you. But yo're my kid, Dan. If you want me, I'm behind you.'

In Dan a sudden warmth broke and filled him. Now he had come home. Now, no matter what happened, he was back where he belonged. The hardness was gone from his eyes and relief sounded in his voice. 'I'll need your backin', Dad.'

Bruce looked up again, and on his face the harsh lines softened. 'You got it, boy!' he rasped. 'Tell 'em to go to hell. Don't answer any questions. You ain't guilty. I'll get the best lawyer in the state, an' we'll tear their case all to hell!'

Dan grinned frankly now. 'We won't need a lawyer,' he promised. 'It's all right. Don't you worry.' He started his horse again, and with Penny riding on one side, Bruce walking on the other, the three approached the porch.

At the hitch rail Dan halted and, dismounting, tied his horse. The trio mounted the steps, the girl and the man still flanking Dan on either side. On the top step Dan

243

paused.

'Penny,' he said levelly, looking at the sheriff, 'told me why you wanted me. I've come in to give myself up.'

'So Penny told you, did she?' Murrah growled. 'Did she say I wanted you for murder?'

'She told me that too.' Dan's voice was steady. 'Let's get inside. It's cold out here.' The group parted and, moving through, Dan held the door open for Nevada and Penny, Murrah halting behind him.

'Go on in,' the sheriff rasped. 'You won't pull a fast one this time!'

Dan crossed the living room and took a chair, Bruce stopping beside his son as though to protect him, and Murrah, legs widespread, towered over Dan and scowled down at him.

'So Penny told you I wanted you for murder,' he grated, 'an' still you had nerve enough to come in an' give yoreself up?'

Penny made a small sound of distress, and Dan reached out his hand to her. 'I didn't kill Carl,' he said steadily. 'I came in as soon as I found out he'd been murdered.'

'You had a fight with Carl just before he was killed,' Murrah blustered, 'an' we've found money from the Stockman's robbery in yore grip. We've got proof yo're guilty, Mar.'

'That money in my grip was paid me on a bet,' Dan said steadily. 'An' I didn't kill Carl. I didn't even have a gun that day. I'll answer

244

questions, Murrah, anything you want to ask me, but first I want Smokey Darnell in here.'

As though in answer to the words, the door banged open and Darnell came in. He stood poised before the door an instant and then, striding over to Dan, snarled his triumph. 'By God, I knew they'd get you, you murderer! I wish I'd been the one to catch you! You wouldn't be sittin' there!'

Murrah pushed Darnell back. 'I'll do the talkin',' he rasped. 'Yo're willin' to make a confession, Mar?'

'I've got nothing to confess,' Dan answered. 'You've accused me of killin' Carl an' of robbin' the Stockman's Bank.'

'And of being one of a gang that traveled with the show and taking part in half a dozen robberies and a murder,' Garza added. 'The mask you lost was found in the hand of a dead man.'

Dan squeezed Penny's hand and released it. 'An' I didn't do any of those things,' he said. 'Let me tell you. I found out that the masks used in Brule came from Ruffin's show. I wrote you that, Murrah.'

'You wrote!' Murrah scoffed. 'Where's the letter? I never got it!'

'I wrote you, just the same.' Dan's voice was calm, and his eyes coolly scanned the room, looking from one man to the next. Every man was watching him intently.

'An' if you ain't guilty, then why did you run

when I arrested you?' Murrah demanded. 'Maybe you can tell me that!'

'Does runnin' make a man guilty?' Dan drawled. 'I lost my head, but I'm not runnin' now. I came in an' gave myself up after you couldn't catch me. Does that look like I'm guilty?'

Purrington nodded slowly, his gray eyes fixed on Dan's face. Dan flashed a glance at the captain and knew that Purrington was with him.

'You wanted to talk,' Murrah snapped. 'You know what yo're accused of. Go ahead an' talk!'

'I will!' Dan straightened in the chair. 'I told you after the Stockman's robbery that I'd seen a little gold saddle watch charm on one of the men. Remember? I told Carl Thwaite about that too. Carl had one of those watch charms, an' Carl saw the masks that were used. He must have known they came from the show.'

Dan paused. Murrah said, 'Well?' a little doubt in his voice.

'Well,' Dan continued, 'maybe Carl got some ideas. Maybe Carl talked to somebody about it. Maybe that's why Carl was killed.'

'Maybe!' Smokey Darnell snarled. 'You killed Carl, you damned murderer! You know you did!'

'No.' Dan shook his head as he stared straight at Darnell. 'I said "maybe", but I didn't mean it. That's what actually happened.

246

Carl had an idea of who had done the business an' he talked to this man. Carl scared him, an' that man killed Carl. He had to, because he knew that Carl would turn him in. He shot Carl an' then beat Carl's head with a rock to make it look like Carl's horse had killed him. He stuck Carl's foot in a stirrup an' turned Carl's horse loose, but before that he did one other thing. He was so anxious to make it look right that he went too far. He dragged a spur across the seat of Carl's saddle to leave a set of tracks. You remember that. All of you. You know there's a set of tracks across the saddle.'

Heads were nodding in the room, Buck, Tom Ruffin, Purrington, all giving confirmation.

'Carl's saddle is out on my horse now,' Dan drawled, still watching Smokey Darnell levelly. 'The spur tracks are on it. They'll fit the spurs of the man who made 'em. *Pull off your spurs, Smokey, an' let us try 'em on those tracks, broken rowel an' all!*'

Dan came to his feet. He had told his story, guessing part of it, piecing out the rest from what he knew. He had seen the battered spurs that Darnell wore, had seen their broken rowel; old spurs, not good enough for show use, left at the ranch during the show season.

Smokey Darnell did not move. His eyes darted to right and left like those of an animal caught in a trap.

'Pull 'em off, Smokey!' Dan rasped. 'Or are

247

you afraid to make the try?' He surged a step forward, and Bruce Mar followed his son.

To Smokey Darnell it must have appeared that the two Mars were about to attempt the thing Dan had commanded. He broke into action, his hand diving beneath his shirt and reappearing, filled with a weapon. One hurried shot he flung at Dan, a shot that whispered past and buried itself in the wall, and then, before a man could move, Darnell had flung open the door and was gone.

Before Dan could reach the door Murrah was in the opening. A shot flung Murrah back and down, blocking the door, holding back Purrington, Buck Ruffin, and Garza. Tom Ruffin fell backward as his rocking chair capsized. Penny screamed and sprang to follow Dan, bumping into Bruce and throwing him off stride. Nevada did not scream but moved swiftly to Tom, bending to help him up; and Dan, jumping over the sheriff, was the first man out. He reached the edge of the porch as Darnell gained his horse. Darnell flung another shot, and Dan dodged. Then Darnell was pounding away on his frightened horse, and Dan ran down the steps. His horse pulled free as Dan reached the hitch rail, but Dan caught the flying reins and jumped for the saddle. Purrington, Bruce Mar, Buck Ruffin, all came boiling out to the porch. Bruce and Buck Ruffin ran down the steps and, mounting their horses, followed Dan; and from the bunkhouse and cookshack Ruffin's cowhands came running, brought by the sound of the shots. On the porch Purrington slowly lowered the gun he held. There were too many in the way for him to shoot; then from the living room Tom Ruffin came, supporting Murrah.

Darnell had almost reached the draw. Dan was nearly there, and halfway between draw and house Buck and Bruce Mar thundered after the two horsemen ahead. Smokey turned in his saddle, and a flat report beat back to those on the porch. They saw Dan drop low in his saddle. They saw Smokey's horse go into the draw and come scrambling out on the other side. They saw Dan reach the draw and disappear, and Smokey, atop the farther bank, wheel his mount and bring his arm level to shoot once more.

'God!' Purrington exclaimed. 'He can't miss. He can't!' The captain whipped up the gun he held and fired twice. Dust kicked up on the bank of the draw, and Darnell, having fired, lifted his arm as though in salute and rode off toward the east. In the draw there was motion, and then Dan's horse came scrambling up the bank bearing a hatless rider, reached the top, and followed after Smokey.

No one spoke on the porch. Men held their breaths, and Penny made a small whimpering sound as Nevada's arm closed around her. Before them a drama unfolded. They saw the horses close, saw Darnell look back and fire again, saw him turn and bend low and beat at his mount with an empty gun, and they saw Dan Mar, straight in the saddle, hatless and his coat flying. It seemed as though the gap between the men remained constant, that neither horse could outdistance the other. And then Dan's arm lifted above his head and swept in swift circles.

'God!' Purrington rasped again.

* * *

Between house and draw Dan bent low and urged his horse for every bit of speed. He rode a top cow horse of Ruffin's cavvy, but so, too, did Smokey Darnell. Dan saw his quarry turn, saw Darnell's face with the lips drawn back in a snarl. He saw the gun in Darnell's hand, saw it bounce, and something whispered past him. Then Darnell's horse dropped into the draw.

When Dan reached the draw Darnell was across. Dan saw Smokey turn and poise the gun, and it seemed that Dan was staring directly into the muzzle. Lead slugged at him, scalding across his thigh, making his horse flinch and jump. Dan kicked with his spurs, forcing his mount up the bank. He did not see or feel Darnell's second shot. Atop the bank the distance closed a little; Darnell's deliberation had paid a dividend. The space closed a fraction, a little more, and then seemed fixed. Under him Dan's horse began to labor.

He could not reach that other horse, could not get to him. There were fifteen feet between them, and Dan could not cross it. Rage filled the boy, anger at himself and at his horse. He spurred and cursed, but slowly the distance widened, inches at a time. Smokey Darnell was getting away, Smokey Darnell who had killed Carl, his friend.

Dan could not reach Darnell, could not tear him from the saddle, could not drag him down. But wait! There was a way to span that gap, a way to reach across it.

Dan's fingers fumbled with his rope strap and the rope came free. One end was tied hard and fast to the saddle horn. There was a loop in the other end, a loop that grew and sang in Dan's hand as he circled it. The rope shot out. The loop dropped fair and true about Smokey Darnell's neck, and Dan's mount, trained rope horse that he was, braked with sliding hind feet, squatted and sat down.

Under Dan's hand the rope jerked tight, singing like a fiddlestring. Smokey Darnell's horse went on, but Darnell himself, snapped from the saddle, caught like a calf at branding time, jerked into the air and came down. Dan dropped from his horse and ran forward, reached the man, bent, and then, straightening, walked two slow steps toward his horse. There was no need to fall on and hold Smokey Darnell. Other hands than Dan's were holding him, would hold him so forever.

Bruce and Buck Ruffin came thundering up, vanguard of the avalanche. Both dropped from their saddles and ran forward, Buck to Smokey Darnell, Bruce to his son. There was blood on Dan's leg where the bullet had grazed, and his eyes were dazed with shock. He stared at his father with no recognition in his eyes.

'He's dead! I didn't mean to kill him. I wanted to catch him an' bring him back!'

Bruce's arm shot out and caught his boy's shoulder. 'Yo're hurt!' Bruce rasped. 'Yo're bleedin', Dan.'

The first of the runners from the bunkhouse reached them.

They carried Smokey Darnell back across the draw and laid him on the porch. The rope mark encircled Darnell's neck and his head was queerly twisted. Bruce drew Dan into the house, and Penny, white-faced, followed them. The others clustered around the body, and Tom Ruffin put his big arm protectively about Nevada's slim shoulders. Through that group Belle Darnell came, and men stepped back to give her space. She dropped beside her husband, and for an instant all was still. Then Belle lifted the body gently, and her voice was the low, small whimper of a wounded child.

'Smokey ... Smokey ... it wasn't worth it. All the money in the world wasn't worth it. I told you we shouldn't come back here. I told you!'

The men stood awkwardly, eyes averted from the grief-stricken woman, and, in Ruffin's arms, Nevada's shoulders shook. Belle held her husband's body close, and her voice went on, dreeing her weird, crying her hurt: 'Smokey ... Smokey ...'

CHAPTER EIGHTEEN

The train was late, and Art Murrah and Emil Garza sat waiting in Brule's depot. Murrah, his arm in a sling and shoulder and armpit bandaged where Darnell's lead had cut, bit off the end of his cigar as he sat down; and Garza, settling himself on the bench beside the sheriff, struck a match and lighted both cigars. He puffed a time or two and then smiled wryly.

'Well,' he said, 'I'm going back to work. Recently I've been thinking I'd better give up this business and take to farming.'

'It makes a man feel that way.' Murrah grinned around his cigar. 'Still, you were right about one thing: It all boiled down to Ruffin's show.'

'I can't figure how I made that mistake,' Garza said. 'I believed Mar was guilty and, and I couldn't get rid of the idea. Not even after Nevada told me that Mar had pulled me out from beneath a bunch of mules.'

'What about me?' Murrah removed his cigar

253

and looked at it. 'We found that bullet in Carl's head an' Dan ran away. I was sure he'd killed Carl. I went at that business wrong. If I'd questioned Dan instead of arrestin' him, we'd have saved a lot of hard ridin'.'

'If I hadn't tried to put handcuffs on him, Mar wouldn't have run,' Garza said. 'I don't take any credit for this case. I did everything wrong from start to finish.'

'But we got it settled,' Murrah said with satisfaction.

'Because we had a lot of luck. Suppose Darnell hadn't hidden that money from the Stockman's Bank out at Ruffin's? Suppose he hadn't come back to get it? Suppose Mar hadn't discovered that Thwaite's spurs didn't fit those tracks across his saddle or that Darnell hadn't dug out those old spurs to wear when he rode with you? Most of it was luck, that's all I can say.'

'Yeah, we were lucky,' Murrah agreed. 'Sure, we were lucky. I've been sheriff a long time, an' I've found that most of it's luck an' hard work. Dan knew about those spur tracks an' he'd of told me. I'd have kept pluggin' away. I expect I'd have caught up with Smokey.'

'Darnell's wife might have confessed,' Garza said thoughtfully. 'I don't know. She loved the man but she was afraid of him. And she said that he was a woman chaser. She was jealous of him.'

'Yeah,' Murrah drawled. 'Belle knew about Smokey killin' Carl too. She told us that he'd threatened to kill her when they had a fight about Penny bein' in their act. He said he'd killed one man, an' they wouldn't hang him any higher for killin' her too. Remember?'

Garza nodded gravely.

'We'd have got him all right,' Murrah assured. 'It might have taken more time, but we'd have got him.'

'Well'—Garza puffed thoughtfully—'Mar saved us a lot of trouble, anyhow. He had things thought out just as I did, but he'd picked a different man.'

'Smokey must have got hold of the letter Dan wrote me,' Murrah said. 'That's the only way I can figure it. An' when those two toughs jumped Dan they were tryin' to get rid of him.'

Garza nodded. 'It would have been a lot easier if Purrington hadn't shot so straight,' he commented. 'I had Nixon and Hart caught in Willow Bluffs, and then the captain killed them.'

Murrah was pursuing another line of thought. 'Halsey knew that Smokey had given Dan that money,' he stated. 'That would have cleared Dan. An' I'd have gone after Darnell as soon as I found that out. I tell you, Garza, a crook always makes a mistake.'

'Darnell made several.' Garza knocked ashes from his cigar. 'Did you see Dan yesterday? He was in town.'

'Came in to get a marriage license,' Murrah said. 'Yeah. I saw him.'

'How was he feeling?'

'About killin' Smokey?' The sheriff puffed a time or two. 'I don't know. I talked to Bruce, an' he said that Dan was pretty low for a while. Bruce said he had to talk pretty straight to him. I don't know. I never felt bad about killin' a man that had it comin', an' Smokey Darnell had it comin' if a man ever did. Dan will get over it. Penny will make him forget it.'

Garza nodded. Outside the depot a whistle wailed, and both men got up. 'Here comes my train,' Garza stated. 'Well, Murrah, it's been a pleasure to work with you. If you come East be sure to look me up.'

Murrah shook hands with the Pinkerton man. 'An' if you get out this way again an' need some help, I'll be glad to give you a lift,' he said.

The eastbound limited halted outside the depot. Garza took his grip and, Murrah accompanying him, went to the platform. Red Halsey, disheveled and bleary-eyed, descended from the smoking car on the front of the train.

'There's Red now,' Murrah said. 'So long, Garza. Take care of yourself.'

'Good-by, Sheriff.'

A porter took Garza's grip, and he climbed the Pullman steps. Murrah advanced on Red Halsey.

'Boooard!' the conductor called, and lifted his hand.

'Where have you been?' Murrah demanded of Red. 'We could have used you around here a week ago.'

'Where have I been?' Red glared belligerently at his questioner. 'Drunk. An' what's it to you?'

The limited creaked as the wheels began to turn. Slowly it gathered headway, sliding past the depot.

The smoke of the eastbound limited was visible from the porch of Ruffin's ranch house, a black smudge against the blue sky and snow-whitened horizon. Tom Ruffin and Nevada, standing on the porch, did not heed the smoke. The MY buckboard was drawn up below the steps, and from the house came sound of progress as Bruce and Dan Mar brought Penny's trunk downstairs.

'Well, Nevada?' Ruffin said.

'Well, Tom?' Nevada smiled up at the big man beside her.

'It looks like you'd have to get another pardner next year.'

'That's what it looks like.'

'Don't you care?' Ruffin's eyes searched the woman's face.

'Not any more,' Nevada answered honestly. 'I did for a while but I don't now. Dan's right for Penny and Penny's right for Dan.'

'Who are you goin' to work with next season?' Ruffin asked.

'Dan gave me Domino. I'm going to train

257

him this winter. He won't be as good as Gold, but I'll have an act, Tom.'

'Mmmm,' Ruffin said. 'Well, it's somethin' to do. Goin' to be pretty quiet around here this winter. Just you an' Cap an' me, unless Red an' some of the boys get back. Penny gone. Dan gone. Smokey dead, an' Belle takin' him back home to bury him. You were pretty swell to stick to Belle the way you did, Nevada.'

Nevada flushed faintly at the praise. 'Somebody had to help her,' she reminded.

'An' you did it,' Ruffin said. 'You know, Nevada...'

'Yes, Tom?'

'I told you one time you didn't have to work unless you wanted to. That still goes.' Ruffin's face was red.

Nevada put her hand on Ruffin's arm, and the man covered it with his big palm. 'Will you wait awhile, Tom?' Nevada asked.

'I'll keep on waitin',' Ruffin said gruffly. 'There's one thing you want to remember, Nevada. Yo're show people an' so am I. Show people ought to stick together.'

'Show people,' Nevada said, and smiled. 'You're right, Tom. They have to stick together.'

Dan backed out on the porch, carrying the front of Penny's trunk. Bruce followed. 'Set it down a minute, Dan,' he commanded. 'The blame thing's heavy.' They lowered the trunk and Bruce sat down on it. 'Women,' he announced, 'must pack lead in their trunks. Ain't that right, Tom?'

'They pack somethin' in 'em,' Ruffin agreed.

'Penny has clothes in that,' Nevada informed them. 'And she's going to need them all.' She smiled at Dan. 'I helped her pack them.'

'Yeah.' Bruce got up. 'Well, you folks will be over Monday, won't you? You won't forget?'

'Forget?' Ruffin rasped. 'When I'm supposed to give away the bride, an' Buck is best man? I'll say we won't forget.'

'And I'm the bridesmaid,' Nevada said. 'I promised Penny I'd help her dress.'

'Well,' Bruce said apologetically, 'I just thought I'd remind you. Ready, Dan?' Bruce got up from the trunk. 'Let's get this thing loaded. Wait till I get my end up ... There!'

The trunk went down the steps and was lifted to the buck-board. Bruce climbed to the seat while Dan pushed the trunk well forward. 'See you Monday,' Bruce called.

Dan came around the buckboard. He smiled at the two on the porch. 'Come over early,' he urged. 'I'm goin' to need all the help I can get.'

'We'll be over early,' Nevada assured, and Dan climbed up. The buckboard team, impatient, moved ahead as Dan settled in the seat.

'I hope,' Nevada said softly, 'that they'll be happy, Tom. I hope they'll be very happy.'

Ruffin closed his hand on Nevada's fingers.

'They will,' he assured. 'They'll be all right, an' they'll get along with Bruce. Did you notice, Nevada, Dan was drivin'?'